Coveting the First

W. L. Samuel

authorHOUSE®

AuthorHouse™
1663 Liberty Drive
Bloomington, IN 47403
www.authorhouse.com
Phone: 1 (800) 839-8640

Published by AuthorHouse   02/10/2017

ISBN: 978-1-5246-7156-3 (sc)
ISBN: 978-1-5246-7155-6 (e)

Library of Congress Control Number: 2017902107

Print information available on the last page.

This book is printed on acid-free paper.

Also by W.L. Samuel
Touching Widows
Poetry - From My Mind To Yours

And coming next: Victim 69

Acknowledgement

To all my love ones
To the cover models
To all my fans
I appreciate you, thank you for
pressing for this one.
Enjoy.

Prologue

It was 5:30 AM, Jean-Pierre Isaac was alone on one of Antigua's 365 beaches. One for each day of the year, he recalls the Minister of Tourism boasting. Jean-Pierre stood at the shores of Deep Bay feeling the warmth of the water caress his ankles as he looks at its gentle flow. So gentle it did not form a crest, and gave the illusion of stillness under the birth of a new day.

The sun has not yet risen; and as Jean-Pierre stepped further into the water he looked up at the fading dark and the stars that will vanish with it from the might of the Caribbean sun.

Chest deep, he held his breath and submerged. Forty seconds later he came up for air. Seven times, he thought to himself, seven times before the sun rises. As he went under for the second time, he thought about the reason for his first visit to the little island of one hundred and eight square miles.

Chapter 1

THE KAWASAKI NINJA turned off of the main road, Concord Street, and through the arched entrance of University Gardens. A gated community for the rich, and home for the Isaacs, Jean-Pierre and his parents Patrick and Jeanine.

The security on patrol recognized the bike and gave a friendly wave. As usual, the rider popped a wheelie in response.

The streets of University Gardens were almost clear of cars. The majority of its residents parked in their driveways or garages. Passing street signs with names like President Drive and millionaire Ave became so familiar to the Kawasaki rider, they were almost forgotten, like the beautiful lawns to match their mansion-type homes. An outer appearance of perfection, nothing unkempt. An appreciation of this community is sometimes felt by its wealthy dwellers, but it never fails to take the breath away from visitors as their eyes meet the palatial surroundings.

The motorcycle turned into Diamond Street, a cul-de-sac with a circular ending. In its center stood a fifteen feet marble statue of an artist depiction of an angel sitting on the globe. As he throttled down, the rider pulled into the driveway of house number 59 and halted in the garage. After his dismount he removed his helmet, exposing his odd eyes, one blue the other gray.

Stepping through the side door from the garage he entered the foyer, tossing his keys on the table designated for the precious vase which sits on it. Alerted by the sound of keys, the four feet eleven inches figure of a woman rose from her seat in the entertainment room. Her little feet made quick steps to the arched entrance which connects the foyer to the entertainment room.

"Bonjour Jean-Pierre" she said in a tender voice.

"Bonjour mama" he said equaling her tone. Then he caught that look of disapproval in her eyes. Making an about-face, he went to pick up his keys off of the table and placed them on a hook on the key rack next to it. And as if he was reading her mind, he said "there is a place for everything, so everything should be in its place" then he smiled. And she smiled back at him.

He followed her as she sauntered to the entertainment room. The room was modern, furnished with a 60" plasma T.V which connects to the speakers of the stereo system, giving a surround sound movie theater effect to the room. The custom made black leather sofa was crescent shape with a seating capacity of fourteen and three pieces of glass coffee table also crescent shaped stationed before it.

"Is Ana home?"

"Yes, she is in the kitchen, are you taking her to class"

"bien sûr (of course), is she ready?"

"She has been ready, in fact she was calling a cab, but I convinced her that you were on your way. So she decided to fix a snack and wait."

Jean-Pierre said nothing more, looking at his watch he knew his fault. He motioned towards the kitchen but Ana was already entering the room.

"So, you are finally here" Ana said slowly, making sure she pronounced the words as she should, however, unable to mask her Spanish accent.

"mejor" he said, replying in perfect Spanish.

"Don't try to flatter me, you are late, and stop speaking my language to me, I want my English to get better."

"Okay- Okay, but Spanish is the language of romance."

Jeanine looked at him sharply, but it was Ana who spoke up.

"I remember you telly me French is the language of romance."

"Not 'telly', tell, and its past tense so it's told, and…"

Jeanine cuts in, "Clever of you to switch to lessons in grammar, but your treachery is exposed, I think now is a good time for you to make your exit and take Ana to class."

With a heart melting smile Jean-Pierre went and sat next to his mother, kissed her cheek and said "I'm not a traitor je suis francais". His voice smooth and manipulative but sincere. She turned to meet his eyes, then held his hand and patted it, a gesture of acceptance followed by her own warm smile. "You better get going before Ana gets annoyed, and drive carefully."

"I'm taking the bike, it's better for traffic"

"In that case be double careful"

"I'm always careful mama"

Feigning anger Ana threw on her backpack and reverted to Spanish, "ya tu sabe no me gusta que maquina." (You already know I don't like that machine) Then in English again "But I'll be late, so let's go"

Turning to Jeanine, Ana said bye-bye and stormed through the foyer to the garage. There she waited impatiently, donned in the extra helmet she took from the shelf. Jean-Pierre hurried out, started the bike and turned it around. He revved and looked over his shoulder to watch her mount. Unconsciously his eyes travelled the contour of her hips to the curling black hair escaping the base of her helmet, and down again to the shape revealed by her pair of Levis. What Jean-Pierre did not notice was the smile hidden behind Ana's helmet. She smiled for more than one reason, first – because she observed him taking notice, second- she had a secret crush on him and being on the bike were the only times she would get to hold him.

Ana mounted and wrapped her arms around him tightly as if terrified. Jean-Pierre revved again and they left 59 University Gardens.

At a window Jeanine watched her son as any concerned mother would. But her fear was quelled with her thought of how specially perceptive he was in anything he engaged. They were gone, but she stayed staring out of the window. Her reverie taking her back to her son's childhood.

*****

The year -1981- Jean-Pierre was six years old, sitting around the table eating his favorite cereal, Frosted Flakes. His father Patrick sat across from him and slowly sipped his tea. Patiently, he waited for his son to finish so he can carry him to school. Jeanine also sat at their five-piece table set, but she was not eating. Instead, she was pondering on a sequence of numbers as she filled out a New York Lottery ticket. Even at this young age Jean-Pierre was very sensitive. Concerned for the bewildered expression on his mother's face, he asked "qù est-ce qùil ya mama" (what's the matter mom). His French was fluent and his father was impressed by him. For he himself was mediocre in the language, never taking heed to his wife to practice her native tongue.

"Nothing dear" She answered in English, so Patrick would not feel left out of the discourse.

"Just some numbers I'm thinking of in hope of winning tonight's lottery."

"Then you have to use 3, 9, 18, 21, 27 and 33" said Jean-Pierre, spacing the numbers as he said them slowly.

"Oh just great!" Patrick exclaimed "you've been teaching our son to gamble" he said, clearly upset at the notion.

"No Patoe" she protested, using the pet name she gave him. "It's the first time he's participating." Patrick scrutinized his wife and son then asked "so how did he know to pick only six numbers"

Immediately Jeanine answered "I don't know". Then curiously she looked at her son to ask, but before she could, he said "They just came to me". Then he continued to eat, trying to hurry for his dad to take him to school.

Fifteen minutes later, Jean-Pierre and his dad stood at the door of their cozy apartment and waited for Jeanine to do her ritual inspection. She corrected her husband's tie even when it did not need correcting. And straightened her son's collar even when it did not need straightening. Then they would both receive a kiss from her and would hear her say –"vous avez bonjour" (have a good day). It was always said in French for the benefit of Jean-Pierre. Oh yes – when jean Pierre was just a tot, Patrick insisted that Jeanine speaks English to him. But she stood her grounds and said he will have enough people talking to him in English when he starts school. Then she added with a hint of venom in her voice-"when my son speaks French, he must sound French, not like an American imitating French" with that, Patrick yielded to the will of his wife.

They were gone now, Patoe to his accounting job with Einstein & Goldberg, and Jean-Pierre to Public School 95. Right away Jeanine made herself busy with cleaning their small apartment which was located at the corner of Jamaica Ave. and 185th Street in Queens New York.

Unlike most stay-at-home moms, after her domestic chores, Jeanine did not get lost in day-time talk shows and soap operas. However, she did get lost, she had an obsession for mystery novels. And when she's buried in them, she would lose all sense of time and reality. Hence the reason for her to set the alarm to remind herself of the time to pick up her son from school.

Jean-Pierre loved the afternoon walks home with his mom as much as he loved the morning drives with his dad. On their route, just a half block from home, Jeanine made their usual stop at Moore Snacks Convenient Store. She gave Jean-Pierre a quarter and he went straight for the video game while she purchased a Hostess Twinkie for him and the lotto tickets for herself.

"Good afternoon Mr. Moore"

The dark skinned man was in his sixties, seated on a stool behind the counter. His moustache matching his silver rimmed glasses. Peeping over the rim he said- "Oh- Mrs. Isaac, how are you"

Before she could answer he glanced at the game machine and added

"He sure loves that game"

"Yeah, that Pac-whatever-you-call-it" she said with a twist to her mouth

"Pac-Man, and all the boys seem to love it, even me" Moore said with a grin.

Moore let his nephew take the cash register and continued his chit-chat. After fifteen minutes, Jean-Pierre went to his mother and interrupted her for another quarter, stretching his please- "pleeeease" But her answer was the same as always.

"Tomorrow is another day, or would you prefer the extra game now and no snack tomorrow"

He would always choose to be wise. Jeanine was not sure however, if his wisdom came from not wanting to part with his Twinkie treat.

Later that evening after the 10 o'clock news, they announced the winning numbers. Jeanine was dumbfounded, her fingers trembled with the ticket between them. She tapped Patoe to get his attention, speechless and wide-eyed she pointed to the ticket, then to the television. Back and forth she pointed until Patoe broke the silence.

"Oh my God-Oh my God" he said in shock but keeping his voice just between him and his wife.

Then she found her voice "yes- we WON!" she couldn't help to scream out the last word. Then Patrick still in his state of shock started to mumble the figures.

"Fifteen- fifteen-oh my God fifteen"

"Yes Patoe, fifteen million"

*****

Jeanine was pulled from her trance when she saw the jaguar drive up the driveway. Slowly, she closed the curtain and made her way to the kitchen.

"Honey, I'm home" Patrick hollered out, a habit he picked up 19 years ago, when they bought the house. A proud owner who always wanted to mimic the husbands of the many t.v. sitcoms. But his life was not a comedy, and he was truly happy to get home and say those words after a long day at Isaac, Einstein & Goldberg Accounting.

"Hello Patoe my darling, how was your day?" Before he answered, he looked at her curiously, wondering for a split second about the date and if he is forgetting any special occasion. No-he thought, then responded. "Fine, oh we got a new account today, we have a three year contract with Long Island General Hospital to handle their internal audits. The Board suspects' misappropriation, but they can't just fire their chief accountant without evidence, or they will have one hell of a lawsuit on their hands. So, how was your day?"

"As usual, accept I didn't have Ana prepare dinner." Before she could finish what she was say, he thought he had the answer to his suspicion in her greeting, so he blurted out with a little excitement "Oh, you want to go out for dinner?" Jeanine looked at him blankly, then said, "no dear", then added with a smile "Its better." Patrick did not answer, but just watched her and allowed her to continue.

"I cooked," with sparkle in her eyes. "I didn't want you to forget that your wife is still able" she added with emphasis on the words wife and able.

"I have not forgotten" he said casually, adding "so what are we having?"

"Go and freshen up, and when you return, the table will be set."

Twenty minutes later, showered and dressed in a knee length black silk kimono with golden dragon designs on the cuffs and the back, Patrick hurried to the dining area, not wanting to keep Jeanine waiting. She was pleased to see him in the gift their son brought back from Japan. On Jean-Pierre's last visit to Tokyo he bought them his & hers matching kimonos.

The table was arrayed with a combination of Antiguan and Guadeloupian cuisine, birth place of Patrick and Jeanine.

"Wow" Patoe said, filled with mouthwatering excitement.

"I know" Jeanine said, smiling up at him.

The meal contained callaloo, a dish made primarily of spinach and okra – well seasoned and blended after it is cooked – resulting to a very thick soup-like dish. There were sweet-potato-coconut dumplings about a ½ inch thick and 3 inches in diameter, lobster and crab with homemade garlic cream dip, spanish mackerel in tomato sauce, and fungee balls – a dish made from cornmeal, assorted steam vegetables and potato salad. For drinks, she prepared a Caribbean beverage called ginger-beer.

Enjoying the food and each other's company, along with Phyllis Hyman softly playing in the background, Patrick thought it was a good time to discuss Jean-Pierre.

"So, did you try to convince our son to hire a full-time manager for his store so he can come on board at the firm? Because I tried, and he's not listening to me."

"No, there's no need, he already has a full-time manager. He's simply not interested in working for anyone Patoe darling, so don't take it personal."

"It's just that he has a gift with figures, I don't want it to go to waste."

"It's not wasted, he is his own boss and he's doing well. Not to mention- he travels to those trade shows with new inventions all the time."

"I know, but working with the firm would not hinder his travel. I know it's for his business."

"Let it go Patoe, he enjoys what he does and he enjoys being the head." With that said, Jeanine took a bite of dumpling dipped in callaloo.

"Okay, I guess you're right. By the way, did he mention a date for the wedding?"

Jeanine almost choked and cleared her throat with a gulp of ginger beer before she answered. "What wedding?" She asked, surprised by the information.

"Isn't Sharon seven months pregnant?"

"Well- um, yes" Jeanine answered, and realized how much attention Patrick actually paid to the timing of the pregnancy.

"Don't you think he should do the proper thing and marry her?"

"We can't make him marry anyone, whenever he's ready I'm sure he will let us know. Besides, he told me she moved into his penthouse."

"Oh- OK, a sign of commitment. But wait a minute, didn't he spend most nights here last week?"

"Yes, and when he wasn't here he was with Domonique." said Jeanine, letting the cat out of the bag. Patrick was the one who was now stunned. He didn't mind his son sailing around before deciding which water is best to anchor his ship, but he was totally against the irresponsible act of getting a woman pregnant, then leaving her to tag another.

"So this is what we've taught him, to be a baby-daddy. What's wrong with Sharon? She seem to be a nice young woman. Being wealthy should make him more careful, not less. And who is Domonique?"

"I agree with you that Sharon seems to be nice, but Jean-Pierre is not a fool. He's worth millions and Sharon will automatically be entitled if they were to marry. Perhaps he's waiting to see if she is worth it. There's nothing wrong with waiting. As for Domonique, all I know is she speaks French and our son is fond of her. Now let's forget Jean-Pierre, he's a smart young man, I want us to continue to enjoy our night."

Patrick released a sigh in agreement "my dear, you're right" Then he stuffed his mouth with mackerel and dumpling.

"And when I say enjoy our night, I mean prenons plaisir la nuit" she ended in French, knowing he knew what she meant. Patoe reached across and with the back of his hand, he gently touched her cheek. She knew he was telling her she was beautiful and he loved her. It was what he always did when he said it. But tonight his mouth was stuffed with dumpling, so his eyes did the talking, and she responded in kind, satisfied that phase one of her objective was achieved and that tonight he will make up for three weeks of inactivity. But she knew what troubled him, his birthday is in two weeks, it would make him forty nine. Jeanine is forty six and she thought how accurate the statistics are about men and sexual depression when they come close to fifty. In the same breath she put away the thought, because tonight, she will rejuvenate him.

Chapter 2

JEAN-PIERRE WAS ON the Van-Wyck Expressway, heading to his penthouse in Manhattan. He moved through traffic easily as if mentally connected with the other motorist. He was one with his machine, at full throttle the weight of the motorcycle was imperceptible.

He had taken Ana on time to her six o'clock class at Hillcrest Learning Institute (H.L.I) and now his adrenalin was at peak as he raced to meet Sharon for six thirty.

Under his helmet his ears were tuned to the hum of the engine, his eyes anticipating danger, then suddenly, fifty yards ahead a police cruiser was parked in the emergency-rest lane. Jean-Pierre did not attempt to slow, instead he hit the throttle sending the digital speedometer from 140 mph to 180 mph. As he flew pass the cruiser, he smiled triumphantly, knowing the officer would not give chase after reading his radar and surmising his car was outmatched.

*****

Jean-Pierre parked the Kawasaki at its reserved space next to his BMW X5 in Tony's garage, then began the half block walk to his penthouse at Lexington and 39th street. It was the first week in September, the breeze light and at 6:25 pm the sky had its sunset hue, a red-orange turning to lavender. With his helmet in his hand, Jean-Pierre dressed in his blue jeans and leather racing jacket walked briskly like every other New Yorker, noticing but still oblivious to its usual seemingly calculated chaos. The honking horns, shouts of 'fucking asshole', and busy pedestrians, all seen and heard and still not seen or heard.

The elevator stopped on the 18th floor and Jean-Pierre went to his apartment, number 1805. As he entered, he placed the helmet on the mahogany stand and his jacket on a brass coatrack. The penthouse was everything one would expect it to be, being owned by a millionaire and owner of Tech World. It was plush, with the latest in electronic gadgets, like remote control vertical blinds and voice activated lights.

Stepping further inside, Jean-Pierre sensed something amiss. Where is Sharon? He thought to himself, even if she was napping he would know he had arrived, because the door triggers the chime in the master bedroom every time it opens.

"Sharon" he called out, but there was no answer. "Sharon" he called again in a more concerned tone, making his way through the living room, then down the hall to his room. The door was ajar, he opened it slowly, speaking softly now he said "Sharon". The room was dark, yet he saw her silhouette sitting on the bed, but she did not answer.

"Sharon, are you okay?" he asked anxiously, but still no response.

"Lights dim" he said, and instantly the lights came on, on dim mode.

"Lights off" she said, and they went off as quickly as they came on, but not before Jean-Pierre noticed the glitter of a tear drop on her cheek.

He sat next to her, and in his most attentive manner, placing his hand on hers, he asked "Why are you crying?"

"I'm leaving"

His heart seem to skip a beat. "What do you mean you're leaving?" he asked baffled by her suddenness.

She gave an enigmatic chuckle, then said "You speak eight languages, and don't know what..." Then her voice became louder "I'M LEAVING MEANS!"

Jean-Pierre tried to contain his frustration by speaking calmly, not wanting to further agitate the situation. "Why are you leaving?" he asked. There was a moment of silence, then she started.

"I never asked to come here. I was content in my own apartment. It was you who insisted that I move in with you. It was you who insisted I take leave from my job until the baby is born. I am an independent woman, but I listened to you and gave you what you wanted, because I love you and I thought it was best for our baby."

And now the tears flowed, but Jean-Pierre said nothing, he stayed silent knowing she had more of her vexation to vent.

"You've been avoiding me like I have the plague, I've been here for two weeks and for a whole week you did not sleep home! I don't want to chase you from your home, so I'm leaving. My apartment hasn't been rented, so being it's available, I'm moving tomorrow. Now you can sleep home and invite that bitch into your bed."

Her last sentence stuck him like a needle, he wanted to remain quiet, but couldn't let her continue without his rebuttal.

"Is that what this is all about, Domonique? She has nothing to do with us"

"If you think it's all about her, then you haven't been listening. You never lied to me J. P, so from the beginning I knew I wasn't the only woman you were with. The choice was mine and I accepted those conditions. But I thought you started to feel for me as I feel for you, because it was you who suggested to stop using condoms. I thought it was your way of saying you were committing to me."

She wiped her nose and sniffled. This time Jean-Pierre remained silent, allowing her to vent.

"Last month you said you were going to dinner with a customer who had invited you. The following day the same thing. Then I asked and you told me, the customer was Domonique and you slept with her. Good- you didn't lie, but it hurts all the same. And when you asked me to move in with you, even though I protested, I was happy. I believed you were finished with your fling. But I see the truth now and I will not delude myself any longer. You will never commit, there will always be a Domonique popping up."

Jean-Pierre felt it was time to cut in, he couldn't let her monologue continue. He went on one knee prostrating before her, and filled with compassion he said-

"I'm sorry, you mean more to me than I show" then he placed one hand on her abdomen and said – "both of you- so please stay, let me take care of you."

Just when she was beginning to simmer, his last few words sparked the flames. Sharon's voice came back with a venom. "See what I mean, you don't understand, you think I need you to take care of me. I have my own money J. P, what I don't have is my own man, and that's what I want you to think about. But it's my fault, you didn't change, I did. I allowed my heart to go deeper than casual."

"You're not the only one that changed. Just because I don't say what I feel, doesn't mean that I don't feel what I feel- I'm not void of emotions." Then his voice hardened – "I SAID I'M SORRY – NOW DON'T TELL ME HOW I FEEL – AND DON'T THINK ABOUT PACKING BECAUSE YOU'RE NOT LEAVING."

Sharon let out a hysterical laugh before she asked "so what am I, your prisoner?"

"Lights on" he said, and the lights came on bright – exposing his one blue one gray eyes. Giving her a penetrating stare,

Jean-Pierre said with a voice just as piercing – "If you love me as you say you do, then you will stay." Then he turned to walk out, but she held his hand and looked up at him.

"What is that I'm not doing that you want me to do? It's only my seventh month, you can still enjoy me."

"It's not you, it's me. I would never forgive myself if there were complications because of my selfish desire to be satisfied."

"Don't feel that way J. P, my GYN said it is safe for me to have sex. Some women have it down to the last two weeks before delivery."

He touched her face with the back of his hand, a habit he unconsciously picked up from his father was now his way of telling Sharon that he loves her without saying the words. He led her to her feet and kissed her gently on our lips. She was beautiful, her mother was Filipina and she had her mother's eyes and hair texture. Her father was African-American and she had his beautiful dark complexion. Her coiffure was trimmed to her nape and she sported a short bang. Her nose – small but in proportion with her face, her lips full – sensual and always inviting.

His kiss opened her appetite for him, so she opened her mouth and instinctively his tongue found hers. His excitement increased, and traveled to his loins. He started to caress her, slowly he raised her dress and slipped one hand under her panty to massage her buttocks, then slid his fingers down its crevice to find her partially shaved nest and her fluid of readiness.

Removing his hands but not his lips, he gently lowered her back to the bed. He massaged her breasts, and just as he was working his hand to meet the short dark hairs of her pelvis, his hand froze on her abdomen and it began a chain reaction, freezing his whole body.

"It's Okay J. P, I'll be fine" Sharon said, then kisses him to encourage him to continue. But, he did not. And he said nothing, just looked at her with his odd eyes filled with sadness. She reached out to him, understanding now for the first time that in spite of the fact that he may bed others, that it was she who he loved. The thought comforted her and she decided she would do whatever it takes to keep him home. Softly she said "It's alright J. P, we can try again later. You're not going out are you?"

"Oh that reminds me, I have to pick up Ana from class."

Sharon released her embrace and looked at his strong face. His hair cut like a soldier's, his complexion – copper like his mother's, then she spoke with a crisp voice.

"You HAVE to or WANT to? Because if you have to, then go. But if you want to, then I need some air - so I'll be along for the ride. And since we're on the subject, are you screwing the maid too?"

"No Sharon, and that's not fair, you know we don't think of Ana as a maid, regardless of her function she's like family."

"I'm sorry J. P, you're right, but you can't blame me for my woman's intuition. After all, what woman would not be attracted to a handsome man with an athletically built body that spells action?"

Jean-Pierre laughed then said "don't try to flatter me"

Sharon looked into his eyes and he felt the sincerity when she spoke "Not flattery my dear – truth."

Then in a serious but loving tone he responded "If it's truth, then in truth you're my equal." He then helped her to her feet. "I'll call the limo for Ana. Are you hungry?"

"Hungry for what?" Sharon asked, as she pinched him.

"For food."

"Yes, and for everything else."

"You want to go out or order in?"

"Let's go to Little Dragons, it's just a block and I need the exercise."

"Sounds great. I'll arrange Ana's ride while you get ready."

Jean-Pierre went to the phone and pressed the button for speaker and the automatic dial was activated. 'What number would you like dialed?' the computer voice asked.

"Limo service." Automatically the seven digits for Tony's Limo Service were dialed.

Tony's Limo Service was owned by Anthony Padrino, who also owned Tony's Parking Garage.

"Hello, Tony's limo service, how may I help you?" The sweet voice of Cynthia Caldone echoed through the speaker, in a Brooklyn-Italian accent, a voice Jean-Pierre recognized instantly.

"Hello Cynthia, how are you?"

Equally recognizing his, she responded "Oh hello Mr. Isaac, fine thank you and you?"

"Wonderful, just wonderful."

"So what can I do for you?'

"I need Ana picked up for 8:30. She's at H.L.I."

"Will do, I'll send Ronnie right away."

"It's only 7:15."

"It's best to always be early and never late."

"Thanks Cynthia, have a good evening."

"Same to you, Ciao."

The line clicked and another dial tone sounded, Jean-Pierre did not wait for the computerized voice, he blurted out "Ana's cell." The phone rang then went to message service. Good – he thought to himself, she had the courtesy to switch to message service and not disturb the class. "Hi Ana, I will not be able to pick you up so I'm sending the limo for you. I'll call you later."

Just as he hung up he turned to see Sharon dressed in jeans and a sweatshirt. She wore no makeup except for cocoa colored lipstick. She was simple and beautiful.

"Lights off" said Jean-Pierre, then they left the penthouse hand in hand.

Chapter 3

8:40 - PM

DOMONIQUE SALISBURY, AGE 23 sat in her bathtub reading a book her mother gave her. She was five feet six inches tall and carried a figure of 34-18-36. Her mother - a Guadeloupian Indian, her father - was a European tourist who was smitten and married in two weeks.

When Domonique was only a year old, he mysteriously died, so she never knew him. And the only thing her mother ever told her about him was that he was a nice man who left her a trust fund - which she's enjoying now.

Her ivory colored skin shimmered like gold under the glow of candles surrounding the tub. Her hair long and wavy, spiraled over her shoulders to touch the tip of her nipples. Her face was the image of Rosario Dawson with green eyes- catlike in nature. Her fingers carried long nails, not press-on. She was all natural - all beautiful - and all enticing.

Domonique turned the pages slowly, repeating in her mind again and again its contents. She recalled what her mother calls -'the life line'-. "Your power is your life Domonique, but you have to use it to master it." 'Yes' - she thought to herself as she put the book aside and tilted her head back, allowing the heat of the water to penetrate her. 'Yes', she hissed – tonight I will summon Jean-Pierre – just like last night. Then her mind flashed back to their passion.

Domonique's skin was oiled and scented with lavender. She straddled Jean-Pierre and moved her pelvic to the rhythm of his heartbeat. Her fingers clawed at his muscular chest. She leaned forward, kissed him, bit his lip slightly – then his ear, and while his lobe was still between her teeth, she murmured, "Hurt me"

He rolled, putting her under him. Then he held her hair in his hands, keeping her head pressed to the bed. Then he commenced thrusting his hips hard and fast, causing her to shriek. When she did, he did also, and their bodies glistened under the light of three black candles.

*****

Ana Castillo, age 22 peered out of the limousine's window, not looking at anything in particular. Her fingers touched the helmet that sat in her lap. It reminded her of the fear of falling, which was conquered by her excitement and osmotically by Jean-Pierre's confidence.

Her fingers drummed as she wondered if she should ask him to teach her to ride. She giggled at the thought, then focused on the passing street lights and thought how different things are from Columbia.

Ana Castillo has been with the Isaac family for nine months. Her mother Rosa Del Gato Castillo worked for the Isaacs for five years before she convinced Jeanine to help bring Ana to the States. Ana is the youngest of four children. Her father Carlos thought he was cursed for not having any sons. Still, he adored his daughters and worked hard to protect the women in his home. But, he could not. All of Ana's sisters have been raped before the age of fourteen. The oldest – when she was ten, by a friend of her teacher. The second – when she was twelve, washing clothes for a neighbor a mile down the road. And the third – when she was thirteen, she was home alone when two men stopped and asked for water, then decided to help themselves to more than water.

Ana always feared what happened to her sisters would happen to her, but it never did. Her father would always say –"I would die first princesita, you are to stay pure for a husband who is worthy." His words always made her feel like royalty even though she knew they were poor. He would even carry her to work with him to make sure she was safe. Then when she was fourteen, he arranged for her mother to be smuggled to Puerto Rico, where she obtained documents to travel to Florida. Ana remembered his last words to her mother –"Rosa mi amor, hacer lo que se debe para enviar para mi princesita" (Rosa my love, do what you must to send for my little princess.)

Carlos loved his family, he would kill for them, and has. Ana knows of two occasions. The first – it was about two months after her mother left. Her father was drinking with an associate, when his associate made a fatal mistake by letting his tongue reveal what he had in his heart. "You have fine daughters Carlos, if I could afford it, I would barter for Ana." This was when Carlos saw red, not because the comment was uncommon, because it wasn't. In Columbia it's a practice for some poor families to accept compensation for the labor or marital purpose of a young teen, so the rest of the family can survive. Carlos saw red because all he could imagine was his princesita being violated, so out came his knife to end the possibility.

The second – was one day at work. Ana was sixteen at the time, and worked with her father. All the other workers knew to respect her. However, there was one in the bunch that occasionally stuck his tongue out at her and licked his lips. She did not tell this to her father in fear of what he might do. But unbeknown to her and the one who committed this folly, he did see. Eventually this worker took a break to relieve himself. Thinking he was alone, he squatted, and it was then he saw Carlos. An hour passed before he was discovered missing. When he was sought, he was found with his throat cut and tongue pulled through and wrapped around his neck.

Later that night, Carlos said to her "tuvo que hacerse princesita, era el tipo de hombre que consigue lo que quiere a cualquier costo. Habi a protegido su honor, y si debo, lo hare otra vez." (It had to be done little princess. He was the type of man that succeeds at any cost in what he wants. I protected your honor, and if I must, I'll do it again.)

Ana thought of her father's courage, she recalls only five occasions of what men called signs of weakness. But she knew the times she saw him cry was because of love and far from weakness. When her sisters were violated, for each one he cried. When he sent his wife away, he cried. And when he said goodbye to his princesita and knew it would be forever, he cried.

One month after Ana was reunited with her mother, they received news that Carlos and family were murdered. Rosa could not bear the pain of her loss, she told Jeanine "If anything should happen to me, take care of Ana. She is healthy, still virgin, and have good heart. Maybe you can help her find a good husband."

Jeanine agreed, knowing she cannot interfere with destiny. Then three days later, Rosa Del Gato Castillo went on a platform at the Flushing train station and stepped in the path of an oncoming number seven train.

The limo door opened and Ana looked up surprised at Ronald McCoy. She was lost in her thoughts and didn't realize she had reached home. "Are you okay mam?" Ronnie asked in a New York accent, but his 'mam' came with a trace of southern hospitality.

"Yes, thank you." She said as she stepped out, then fumbled with her bag in an attempt to tip him. But Ronnie declined.

"That's okay mam, it's all taken care of. Would you like me to see you to the door?"

"No its okay, have a good night."

"You too mam" Ronnie said and watched her use the entrance to the garage. 'That's one pretty chick', he said to himself before he drove off.

*****

10:30 PM

Jean-Pierre relaxed with Sharon in their bed. The lights were dim and they spoke about everything – from business to the vanilla swiss almond ice cream they fed each other. Not completely satisfied with the strawberry cheese cake dessert they had at Little Dragons. Jean-Pierre opened his mouth to accept a spoonful, but Sharon playfully let it miss his mouth, and dabbed a little on his nose before feeding him. Then she rose up and licked the ice cream off his nose.

"Here" she said, passing him the container then removing her night gown. He laid in the buff with his upper body in a forty five degree angle supported by pillows. She mounted him, sat across his abdomen, then she took back the container.

"Now this is how you eat ice cream" she whispered, before she dipped her finger in and smeared it on and around her nipples. He responded greedily, devouring one side then moving to the next. Then to her neck, and in a husky voice Jean-Pierre said "You're my favorite flavor – mooorre"

Sharon chuckled at his monster impression, then smeared more on her breast and included her neck. She moaned as his mouth deftly removed the ice cream from her erogenous zones. Her nipples were hard and her breathing heavy, she reached behind her to caress him and found him equally excited and ready. She eased herself back from his hungry mouth, straddled his ankles, and placed a spoonful slowly into her mouth, then leaning forward she gave his flagpole a winter-summer feeling. And after three repetitions of winter-summer, she mounted him, giving him her simulated heatwave. Her body was extra sensitive and with every move of her pelvic, she went closer to the edge.

22

Closer, closer, closer – then finally, she fell over. Simultaneously he held her firm and released a guttural moan and she knew she took him with her. She did not want to move or say a word to interrupt the moment. So she rested her head on his shoulders and stayed in the comfort of his arms, while thinking to herself 'yes my love, tonight you will stay home'.

*****

2:00 AM

In her bedroom Domonique stood before a full length mirror dressed in a black negligée with her hair cascading over her shoulders and her eyes glowing from the candle lights. She stretched forth her hands as if reaching for her reflection, then in a low voice she began speaking to herself and every now and again she called out Jean-Pierre's name. If one was peeping through her window, one would assumed she had gone mad, because her lover abandoned her. She did not hold back the expletives, and her voice became louder and louder. Into the mirror she spoke. "Fucking come to me Jean-Pierre, fucking come to me when I call. Feel my desire and come to me. Feel my desire and come NOW!" As she yelled the last word, the candles blew out, and she stood sweating in the dark.

*****

2:10 AM

Dr. Sharon Mia Henderson was awakened by Jean-Pierre's heavy breathing and grunts. She watched his perspiring body for a few seconds and decided not to awake him, but seconds later his eyes opened.

"Bad dream?" She asked, trying to sound soothing.

"No.... just a ....just a ...., I need some air." He got up and motioned towards the closet. Right away Sharon saw his erection and knew whatever dream he had was not a nightmare. Her mind pulled completely from sleep set her on defense.

"It's after two in the morning, where are you going?"

"Just, just for some air" he said incoherently, not sounding convincing. Quickly she got out of bed and reached for the remote, a flick on the switch and the blinds opened.

"If you need air, I'll open the windows." She did not give him a chance to object, she literally ran to the windows and opened them. Then spinning on her heals, she went and intercepted him at the closet.

"Come back to bed" she said as she put her arms around him. Pressing against him, she felt his desire, his frustration and his resistance. He opened his mouth to speak, but she reached up and kissed him deeply, not giving an opportunity for rejection. As their mouths unlocked, she whispered breathlessly "Take me if you need me, but please don't go."

Sharon's words penetrated him, and with his huge hands he held her head and kissed her with everlasting passion. Then suddenly, he broke the kiss and said "I don't want to hurt you Sharon."

"You won't" she said. And in a final attempt to convince him, she went on her knees to give him her mouth. Jean-Pierre moaned as he felt the sweet skill of her mouth, but her sweetness only intensified the flames. Her mouth alone could not extinguish his inferno, so he raised her to her feet, lifted her, and carried her to their bed.

"Stop me if I hurt you" he whispered.

"Just take me" she whispered back. And he did, again and again and again, till his flames died.

*****

4:30AM

Domonique was in front of her mirror seething.

"How could he resist me?" She hissed.

"Because he loves her." She answered herself.

"Then I will teach her not to interfere." She said, then turned and walked away, and without breaking stride, she raised her hand and the mirror shattered behind her.

Chapter 4

7:00 AM

IT WAS A quiet morning at University Gardens. A few residents were just ending their 6:00 AM routine walk, but Ana Castillo was preparing for her routine day. She did not wear a maid's uniform as other maids in the community. Usually she is donned in a black skirt or pants, with whatever top she finds suitable. Today she is dressed in a knee length black skirt and a cream short sleeve cotton shirt that matched her complexion. Taking a minute to stare in the mirror, she affirms her beauty.

Eight years ago, back in 1992 when Ana was just fourteen, many villagers told her she looked like Paola Turbay. The beautiful Columbiana who took second place in the 1992's Miss Universe contest. Ever since then, she gained confidence and believed her father even more when he called her princesita. But here in America, she felt average amongst so many beautiful women, even though she is a natural. For what does it matter to a man if a woman is artificial or not, after all, are they not the ones encouraging so many women to have unnecessary surgeries?

For bigger boobs – a prettier face, and so on – and so on. Then thinking out loud she said "Why are men so shallow?" and left her room to prepare breakfast.

While in the kitchen, the front door opened, then closed. Ana peered out to investigate. "Oh, good morning Jeanine." Jeanine was dressed in a wind-breaker track suit and New Balance runners, with her hair pulled back in a ponytail. She carried two newspapers, the New York Times and El Diario.

"Good Morning Ana" she said with a smile and placed the newspapers on the stand at the bottom of the staircase.

"How was your walk?"

"Just fine, in fact it was lovely." As she was about to go upstairs, she turned and said "Oh, I invited Kathrine for an afternoon cocktail, but we can talk about that after breakfast." Then she disappeared up the stairs.

Patrick was still in bed when Jeanine walked in the room. He was switching from one news channel to the next. As she undressed for a shower, she gibed him – "Can't get out of bed huh, too much for you last night?" Turning to answer her, he became stirred as he watched her step out of the unitard she wore under her windbreaker.

"Actually not too much at all, I was even thinking that starting tomorrow I'll join you in the mornings."

"Oh pa – lease, I'll believe it, when I see it." She said with a dismissal wave of the hand as she made her way to the bathroom.

Becoming libidinous, Patrick's temperature rose. His heartbeat quickened as his eyes locked on Jeanine's swaying hips and dimpled derriere. On impulse his shorts came off, then he jumped out of bed and trailed behind her.

Jeanine was startled to see him, but became excited when she saw what aimed at her. Patrick's desire made him animal – he bypassed the foreplay and turned Jeanine to face the vanity, then ravished her from behind. She gripped the edge of the vanity and caved to his thrust – gladly welcoming him, till the beast in him was tamed.

*****

8:30 AM

Jean-Pierre turned from his cuddled sleep next to Sharon. She was awakened by the movement of his arm from around her. She stretched and stifled a yawn.

"Good-morning" he said and kissed her cheek, then placed his lips on her abdomen and kissed her again. Sharon smiled and rubbed his stubbly head. "Good-morning to you too." She said.

He rolled out of bed feeling lethargic. So he decided to do thirty squats and thirty push-ups, to get his adrenaline going so he can feel a normal sense of alertness. Sharon watched him complete his sets before she asked "What would you like for breakfast? I'm craving eggs."

"I'll get it, I'll fix you something healthy to go with your eggs." He answered, then took quick strides to the shower.

After two minutes, she considered joining him. But, by the time Sharon made up her mind and was stepping out of bed, he was already coming out. Jean-Pierre was the type of man that can shower and dress in five minutes, and look as good as one who takes a half an hour.

He was dressed in a Burberry's pleated navy slacks and a light blue long sleeve polo shirt, with a pair of Hunters Bay black leather shoes. From his closet he extracted a black Bill Blass blazer and hung it on the brass coat rack by the entrance.

While Jean-Pierre made breakfast, Sharon took her shower. By the time she emerged wearing a white terry cloth robe, breakfast was on the table. Which in actuality only took Jean-Pierre 10 minutes to prepare. "Voila, just as promised"

"Thank you, you're a true gent. Sometimes." She said, and kissed him.

Breakfast consisted of boiled eggs with slices of tomatoes, cucumbers, and lightly toasted wheat bread. It was topped off with Jean-Pierre's special energy shake; made with raw oats, raw peanuts, bananas, honey, strawberries and soy milk.

Jean-Pierre finished eating before Sharon, he glanced at his watch – it read ten past nine. "Time to go." He said, then went to the bathroom to rinse his mouth.

When he returned, he kissed her goodbye.

"Wait" she said, looking uneasy.

"What's wrong?"

"I was thinking of going back to work"

"We discussed this, and you agreed to stay home."

"Yes, but I feel so bored staying home alone. Besides, there are a lot of troubled teens out there."

"That's very noble of you, but I think the Board of Ed will survive the absence of one of their psychologist. Honestly Sharon, I don't think it's wise to absorb other's stress at this time. You can call me selfish, but I don't want you going crazy trying to keep others sane."

"But...."

"Na-na – no buts. If you're bored, do like other women who are not financially deprived."

"And that would be..." she looked at him to fill in the blank and expected a chauvinistic answer, like – go to the salon, but he was close.

"Go shopping." He said, then kissed her and went for his blazer. At the door he turned to look at her, winked, then he puts on his Ray-Ban aviator gradient. Not just because they enhanced his image, but they prevented others from seeing his different color eyes. He gave her a thumbs up, then he was gone. Out the door – down the elevator – out the building – then into a cab.

*****

9:15 AM

Back at University Gardens, Jeanine questioned Patrick on his lack of enthusiasm in getting to the office on time. He's normally out the door by eight-fifteen, and his dress code never altered. Not even on a casual Friday he was casual.

"Pato, do you see what time it is?"

He peeped over the newspaper and answered her nonchalantly. "Sure"

She was about to say something but he put the paper down and continued…

"I was just leaving"

"Like that?" she asked with her face frowned, referring to his attire. He was wearing Dockers and a white shirt with its sleeves rolled up to his forearms, no tie and no jacket.

"I decided to finally take advantage of my position. I think it's called perks." He said with a smile then continued with – "I think I might come home early too, in fact, I may even decide to take the rest of the week off."

Putting her arms around him as she walked him to the foyer, she asked – "So what brought on this change?"

He paused, looked down into her eyes and said – "Last night the food was delicious. But you have always been delicious, and I was reminded of what I was denying myself of and what I've been neglecting to do. Which is to enjoy life with you, and I cannot do that in the office."

He gave her a light kiss on her lips then reached for a set of keys.

"Oh – Pato you picked up the wrong keys."

"No – I'm using Jean-Pierre's Porsche. If he comes let him know that he's more than welcome to the Jag." He winked at her, then he was gone.

Chapter 5

11:00 AM

DELANCY STREET, DOWNTOWN Manhattan was riddled with high school students who went to school just to collect their program cards for the first day. Now they were busy window shoppers taking mental notes of bargains in the stores that still carried the popular 'Back to School Sale' sign in their windows.

Unfortunately, not all had buying on their minds. Kleptomania seems to be contagious amongst most teens who travel in a group, regardless of ethnicity or parent's financial status. Such was the case with Michael Cappello, Bobby Rice and Johnny Santiago. Three sophomores from Park West High School who got infected.

"Okay Johnny, we did it already, so the next store we go into – it's your turn." Michael said, followed by Bobby's "Yeah", advocating his statement. But Johnny just nodded in agreement as his heart beats a mile a minute, not wanting to speak to expose his nervousness.

Looking up at the sign for the electronic store, Michael read it aloud "Tech World", then he went inside and they followed.

Inside, there were glass counter display cases on both sides. The manager, Andrew Bridges was at the register ringing up a patron, while the two sales clerks occupied each side assisting other customers.

Meanwhile, Michael and his two friends browsed through the store and ended up at the rear. They perused a rack of sunglasses and each tried on a pair. As they admired themselves in the large seven feet by seven feet mirror, Bobby said jokingly "look at the Terminator without muscles." - referring to Michael, then they all laughed. They were totally unaware of the man on the other side of the two-way mirror smiling with them. But Jean-Pierre's smile suddenly turned into a disappointed grimace as he noticed one of the teens pocketing a sunshade.

Jean-Pierre did not hesitate to reach for the phone on his glass desk to connect with the line in the store. "Andrew, teenager – blue backpack, don't let him leave and bring him to my office please."

"Yes sir" Andrew said, and casually replaced the phone on its receiver while eyeballing the youngster from the corners of his eyes.

In the midst of their jesting, Bobby realized that Johnny did the deed. So he replaced the shades that he had, then without hurry, made for the door and his cohorts followed suit.

Fifteen feet from success, Johnny's palms sweated.

Ten more feet and he's out the door. Eight .... Seven.

"Excuse me"

The sound of those two words coming out of Andrew Bridges mouth sent Bobby and Michael bolting through the door. Johnny was flustered, he didn't know if he was too slow to react or if the big hand was already on his shoulder when he heard the voice. Either way he figured he was caught, besides, his comrades running certainly signified guilt.

With sweating armpits he tried to respond coolly. "Yes" he answered, looking up as he feigned confidence.

"My boss would like to see you in his office." Andrew said with cold eyes. Obviously repulsed by the youth, and at the same time annoyed with himself for not seeing the caper before his boss brought it to his attention.

Inside of the office, Jean-Pierre sat behind his desk looking up at the young man, then he glanced at Andrew and said "Thank you." Andrew nodded, stepped out and closed the door behind him. Jean-Pierre refocused his attention on the young man before him. He removed his Ray-Bans and got the exact reaction expected – a flinch and a gasp – were most people's physical response upon seeing his odd eyes.

"What is your name?"

"Johnny" his answer came without him thinking.

"Johnny what?"

Johnny pondered on being prevaricative by using an alias, but considered he might be searched, then his true identity would be revealed – so why bother.

"Johnny Santiago sir."

"Well, Johnny Santiago, have a seat."

Johnny sat nervously.

"Do you know why you're in my office Johnny?"

"I think so, sir."

"You think so." Jean-Pierre said sarcastically as he pressed a small remote device on his desk, causing the vertical blinds to open and exposed the two-way mirror.

Johnny had a view of the entire store, but his eyes stayed locked on the very place he stood just moments before. He was hoping he was in the office for any other reason than what he knew deep inside. With watery eyes he came out of his denial and accepted the fact that he was – busted.

Reaching into his pocket, Johnny retrieved the shades and placed them on the desk. A tear drop broke its barricade and streamed down his cheek.

"I'm sorry" he said with trembling lips – "please don't call the police."

"I wa...." Jean-Pierre's words were cut off. Johnny's voice came with alacrity, desperately seeking forgiveness.

"Please – please, you probably wouldn't believe but I've never done this before. If my mom finds out she'll kill me. Please don't call the police."

For a minute they locked eyes, then Jean-Pierre broke the silence.

"I believe you, and I'm not going to call the police."

"Thank you sir, thank you."

"But there should be a penalty. What do you normally do after school?"

"Nothing except for homework."

Jean-Pierre leaned forward, resting his elbows on his desk, he placed his left fist into his right palm. Within ten seconds he thought of a solution, then sat back in the chair with his fingers clasped, palms resting on his belly. Then he asked – "On a regular day what time can you get here after school?"

"Between three and three thirty"

"How would you like an after-school job?"

Johnny's eyes opened wide with surprise – "Sure, I would love it, but why would you hire me after what I tried to do?"

"Hire – no, think of it as an apprenticeship, but you will get a stipend. Not for your first week of course. Consider your first week a sort of community service, reparation for your misdeed. And as to why am I doing this, it's the same reason I didn't call the cops. I believe it's your first time."

"Thank you, I don't know what to say."

"You said enough. Here's my card, discuss your apprenticeship with your parents. If there is a problem have them call me."

"Johnny nodded and accepted the card. His eyes quickly glanced at the name of the man he was not introduced to."

"Well Johnny, have a nice day. I'll see you tomorrow."

Johnny took the cue and stood up, but he did not just turn to leave. He extended his hand and said – "Thank you Mr. Isaac."

Jean-Pierre took his hand and shook it, inwardly happy that the lad was perceptive enough to catch his name and exemplified a mannerism of decorum.

Without any further words, Johnny Santiago left the office and exited Tech World with his mind elated. He ignored the doubt that tried to creep in – that little voice that was saying 'this can't be happening, you're not so lucky, wait till tomorrow you'll see'.

*****

12:10 - PM

Andrew Bridges saw the familiar face came through the door. His eyes automatically went to the legs that extended from the olive green leather skirt, which ended about five inches above the knees. Then they went to the form-fitting top which pronounced the pair of breast that seems to whisper – 'touch me' – in the ears of every man, and even some women. Then back to the familiar face with those hypnotic green eyes that were getting closer.

Without saying hello, the honeyed-voice with a French accent asked "Is Jean in?" and as if expecting the answer to be in the affirmative, she did not pause.

"Yes ma...am" Andrew managed to spit out as her stilettoes clicked pass him. His eyes followed her steps, watching the muscles in her calves flex with every stride. The shift in her rump when her hips swayed, and the bounce of her hair in the rhythm of her gait.

For a moment he wondered what shampoo she used. He imagined what if.... No – his imagination cut short by the superiority of her aura. No – definitely no, he thought. Women like her never go for him. He was only lucky in attracting the average or less than average. But that's okay, because those so called averages, they have the best heart, he thought with a smile.

So, who need those magazine-looking, bitch-attitude-carrying, heart-breaking women? Not a need, he thought finally, and said in a voice barely audible "Just a want – just a want."

Jean-Pierre looked up from his desk when he heard the knock on the door. But before he could answer, in walked Domonique Salisbury.

"Aah bonjour madam, si beau."(Good-morning madam, so beautiful.) Jean-Pierre said as he perused her attire.

"Bonjour mon amour et merci" (Good-morning my love and thanks), then she continued in English "But if I was as beautiful as you say, then you would have found your way to my palace last night." Domonique said this with a smile as sweet as her voice. Her English was not distorted by her accent, but in fact, very pleasing to the ears.

"No offence ma chéri (my darling), but I said beautiful, not irresistible." Said Jean-Pierre, verbally denying the feeling stirring inside him. However, Domonique's expression did not change, because his words had little impact. When she looked into his eyes, they betrayed him. She knew she could make him yield to her, even right there in the office if she wanted to.

Walking around the glass desk, Domonique swiveled the chair which Jean-Pierre sat in, giving her clear access to his lap. She then sat on him, and turned to hang her legs over the arm of the chair as she curled her fingers around his neck. Not releasing her gaze, she kissed him then said "We will see about that." Meaning her status of not being irresistible.

"I came to take you to lunch and reservation has been made, so 'no', will not be an acceptable answer."

Silently conceding as he fell under her influence, Jean-Pierre simply puckered his lips, desirous of another kiss.

Chapter 6

12:15 – PM

ANA EXUBERANTLY CARRIED a silver tray filled with enchiladas. She placed it on the coffee table in front of the host and guest. She then offered to refill their glasses with the Jaboulet red wine which sat chilled in the ice-bucket. Skillfully she poured the strawberry-scented, spicy flavored liquid and topped up the glasses. As Ana turned to leave, Jeanine stopped her. Gesturing to the seat she said "Ana darling you're welcome to join us. You don't have to be so formal."

"Thank you, but please to excuse me, I have some things in the kitchen which needs my attention." The words were spoken slowly in Spanish-accented English, but clear and comprehensible. Ana wanted to stay. Conversing improved her practical use of the language, but she thought it appropriate to decline in order to keep her function in perspective.

When Ana was out of ear shot, Kathrine threw a joke at Jeanine.

"I love her mannerism. Let's swap, your Columbian for my Hungarian."

Jeanine's hand froze over the tray of enchiladas, then she looked up slowly. Her face in dismay as she said to Kathrine Palovski in a very serious tone. "Since when did you begin to make slight of the less fortunate?"

Kathrine continued to be jovial and placed a hand on Jeanine's knee as she said – "Don't be so sensitive darling, you misunderstood me. It was really a compliment to Ana. She's not vaunting or obnoxious of the fact that you treat her more like your surrogate daughter than a maid. Unlike Natalya, George and I make her comfortable enough, but she is still a servant. Even though at times I swear she acts like she's the mistress of the house. By the way darling, neither Ana nor Natalya could be classed as 'the less fortunate', as you put it."

"I suppose I did over react."

"Yes, it's that motherly protective instinct you have for Ana."

Jeanine changed the subject – "Kathrine what did you mean exactly, when you said Natalya acts like the mistress of the house? I sensed a connotation in your voice."

Kathrine did not answer right away, she used the moment to sample the enchiladas. "MMM, these are good." She said with her mouth full.

"Yes they are" said Jeanine, as she filled her own mouth then added "We are not changing the subject, so answer the question."

Kathrine Polovski swallowed the enchilada followed by the Jaboulet. After putting down her glass, she took a deep breath and exhaled slowly. With her chin down, eyes fixed to the floor and hands clasped, she began to speak.

"I never caught them in the act, so I suppose you may think that I'm paranoid. It's just little things, but when I put them all together, they become a big thing to me. Like this morning after the walk, they did not hear me come in. When I went to the kitchen for some juice they seemed to be in an intimate discussion. And when they noticed me, there was a sudden silence before they greeted me. Then when they continued to talk, their voices were at an ordinary audible level. Which I believe was a sham. There have been similar instances when I would walk into a room and they would change the conversation or body position if they happen to be standing too close. Then of course, there are the gifts. George bought her a diamond pendant and it wasn't Christmas or her birthday. And get this Jeanine, Natalya thanked me for it and said that George said that I was the one who picked it and it's a gift of appreciation. Don't you see how they're screwing with my head? Now she wears it around the house like it's her birthmark."

"Kathrine, what if it was a gift of appreciation and George did not want Natalya to think it was more than that, so he told her that you picked it."

With a twist mouth Kathrine looked at her friend and said – "Come on Jeanine I know you don't believe that."

"Just trying to give him the benefit of the doubt."

"Well I'm not buying that excuse, it's more likely that he told her to thank me, so she can flaunt it without me wondering where she got it." Kathrine paused for effect, she wanted Jeanine to see eye to eye with her.

Jeanine used the moment to enjoy more Jaboulet. But after the non-response, Kathrine looked Jeanine square in her face in hope of reading the true feelings behind her impassivity as she asked – "So you still think it's all in my mind?"

Musing over the question, Jeanine tightened her lips, forming little wrinkles at the corners. Then she asked a question of her own. "Kathrine..." her voice lowered as if others occupied the room with them, expressing the desire of being confidential.

"... How often does George let his tiger loose to explore your jungle?"

Kathrine let the question sink in before she answered.

"Well... about once per week."

"Hmph, I see why you're worried."

"You do?"

"Yeah. It's pathetic, you two are in your early forties and you settle for once a week."

"Who said it's me who's settling?"

"Oh Kathrine, if you're the problem, it's either you fix it or don't complain."

"I... I don't know what to do. My mind tells me that I want sex, but my body doesn't respond." Kathrine started to sob and mumbled on – "I think there's something wrong with me. I don't feel that tingle anymore. I can't tell the last time I orgasmed and it's nothing that George is doing different than when I use to climax. It's just me, it's just me." She continued to sob and Jeanine put her arms around her and patted her back.

"Shhh, it's okay, George is not having an affair. It's the guilt you feel from rejecting him is what has been playing on your mind. But what you need to do now is to stop blocking him. If the tiger wants to go in the jungle then let it, it's his, or your fears of it roaming another jungle to feast, might become a reality."

After Jeanine spoke these words, she abruptly stood up and went to her library. When she returned to her seat, she had a eureka-look on her face as she handed Kathrine a book titled 'Communication – The Secret to a Successful Relationship'.

*****

12:30 – PM

Tavern In The Sky was a restaurant in the image of a flying saucer with four legs. It stood about fifteen stories high, overlooking Fresh Meadows Park. Three of its legs were designed to be elevators, but in the end, a decision was made to only use two. The roof was fashioned to accommodate four helicopters.

A young couple stepped out of the chopper with their heads down, eyes squinted and moving briskly. Their clothes flapped from the gust of fury from the copter's blades. As they advanced towards the tavern's entrance, the pilot watched the tall man with envy. Wishing it was his own arm around the waist of the woman in the olive green skirt.

Once inside, all external sounds ceased. The whir of motor and blades were instantly replaced by the acoustics of violins. The maître-d greeting them with overwhelming pleasantry. He was just about to address Jean-Pierre when Domonique cut in.

"I have a reservation for two, my name is Domonique Salisbury."

"Aah, but of course madam, right this way please." Then he paused, and looked at Jean-Pierre.

"I was about to explain that your usual table is occupied Mr. Isaac. I was not aware that we would be honored with your presence."

Then in fluent Japanese Jean-Pierre explained that he too was unaware, it was his female companions' invitation to lunch he could not resist.

"Chushoku shotai tada." (Invitation to lunch alone?) The Japanese man asked as he locked eyes with Jean-Pierre, then they both laughed.

Domonique and guest were seated at a table near the green tinted tempered glass. Which gave the illusion from inside looking out, that the building was afloat.

Perusing the menu, Jean-Pierre decided on the steam combo appetizers. Steamed mussels in mustard sauce, steamed dumplings stuffed with shrimp and steamed crab legs in garlic sauce. He then ordered plain white rice with an array of vegetable with the traditional eating apparatus – chop sticks.

Domonique matched Jean-Pierre's order.

*****

12:45 - PM

Manhattan, with its industrious citizens moving to and fro. Some eating and drinking on the go, none paying attention to the very pregnant woman with shopping bags in each had having difficulty opening the door to Tech World.

Andrew Bridges saw the young woman and rushed to her aid. As he opened the door, he greeted her. "Good afternoon Dr. Henderson."

"Good afternoon Andrew." She said smiling and continued with "Just Sharon Andrew, please leave the title for my patients." Andrew simply smiled and nodded to the request for the umpteenth time.

"Is J.P. in?"

"I'm afraid not."

Sharon had an obvious look of disappointment on her face.

"My feet are so tired. Andrew do you mind if I rest in his office?"

"Of course not D... I mean Sharon, let me help you with your bags."

As Andrew walked her to the office he thought of how much he liked Sharon. She respect him, she's not arrogant as presumptuous just because she has a Dr. before her name, or being the boss's lady. She actually waited for my answer and did not just barge in. As they arrived at the office, Andrew set Sharon's bags aside.

"Thank you Andrew."

"Don't mention it" he said, and closed the door and went back to his duty.

Sharon waddled to the chair behind the glass desk. Slouchily she sat, took in a deep breath then released a sigh of relief. Closing her eyes, Sharon smiled as she inhaled again and recognized J.P.'s fragrance. Then in the same breath her eyes opened slowly and the gradual disappearance of her smile was replaced by a frown of perplexity. Another familiar fragrance lingered in the air. Her pregnancy seemed to have made her hypersensitive, enhancing her sense of taste and smell. Sharon knew she was not imagining the scent of Domonique. What disturbed her was why the perfume was still pungent.

Dr. Henderson didn't need to be a great detective to come to the conclusion of the most logical explanation. The idea of her nemesis still being an intimate part of J.P.'s life threw her into turbulence. Symptoms she knew all too well became clear to her. The increased heart rate, the beaded sweat on her cleavage that was revealed by the décolletage she sported and the throb in her head were all signs of anger building up inside.

Dr. Henderson started taking deep breaths. After her tenth repetition of quick in-hold for three- then slowly out, she recited the 'Serenity Prayer.'

"God, grant me the serenity, to accept the things I cannot change, the courage to change the things I can, and the wisdom to know the difference."

With hands pressed on the desk, Sharon's hanging head shook with disappointment. The anger management technique that she has been teaching dysfunctional teens, did not work this time for her. As she Held back rebelling tears, Sharon stood on shaky knees. Then speaking out loud she commanded herself "Get a grip, don't let them see you like this."

Maybe it was self-hypnosis, perhaps it was pride, but Sharon could have won the Oscar for her performance. Making quick strides, she exited the office with a bright smile and addressed Andrew.

"Thank you Andrew, it's amazing how rejuvenated five minutes can make one feel."

"Don't mention it, oh you forgot your bags, let me..."

"No – no, it's quite alright, J.P. can bring them home." Then touching her belly in a circular motion she said – "I have enough load to carry." They both chuckled and after, exchanged pleasant farewells.

Outside of Tech World, Dr. Henderson took a few paces before she spotted and hailed a cab. Once inside, her façade faded. Her sprightly smile and perky voice vanished, as if by a switch, were turned off.

"Where to ma'am?" the driver asked, looking at her through his mirror.

In a somber voice she answered – "Lexington and East-39th Street." Then they were off, blending with the city's traffic.

In the silence of the ride, the rebelling tears broke their restraints and escaped down her cheeks.

*****

1:30 – PM

Jean-Pierre and Domonique rose to exit Tavern In The Sky. As they approached the door, Sotto the maître-d asked – "Was everything satisfactory?" Jean-Pierre opened his mouth to speak, but as if it's a race Domonique cuts in to answer first. "Absolutely splendid, and the dessert – unforgettable." Then she turned to face Jean-Pierre and asked him "Darling, how is it pronounce again?"

He said it slowly in its syllables "su-ama"

"Aah" said Soto "one of my favorites also."

Suama is a sweet Japanese dessert made of gluten free rice flour, sugar and red food dye. It is a traditional dessert of celebration, always made red and white to symbolize the Japanese flag.

At the exit, Jean-Pierre faced Soto then bowed gracefully and said – "Arigato nüsan" (thank you elder brother). Soto returned his bow in the same graceful manner, no words needed to be said. Domonique looked on, observing the enigmatic bond between her lover and the Japanese man.

Once inside the helicopter, her curiosity led her to enquire – "So, it seems like you and the maître-d have known each other for a long time."

Jean-Pierre didn't quite know what Domonique was searching for, so he kept his response to her statement concise. "Language – ma chéri (my darling), it breeds enmity or friendship."

"So, because you speak his language, you two became friends."

"You can say that."

But what Jean-Pierre did not mention was, the year he spent in Japan to learn the language, he embraced the culture and attended the school of master Jukata to learn the art of kendo. And conversations with Soto revealed that he too was a student of master Jukata. By culture, that makes them brothers in the art.

"Yeah you can say that." He repeated as he begins to feel the tingle from the wine.

Domonique sagaciously observed his relaxed state of mind and closed in on her plan.

"Jean-Pierre." She said alluringly, "I have the second part of your dessert at my palace." Jean-Pierre gave Domonique a half smile, then with half-closed eyes he looked into her green eyes and they pulled him in. She kissed him and it reminded him of the kiss in his office earlier that afternoon and how he wanted more.

Entranced by her kiss, he was oblivious to the fifteen minutes flight time and the landing of the helicopter on the roof of Domonique's penthouse. She held his hand gently yet persuasive as she led him to her suite. Before he knew it, he was naked in her bed. A look of bewilderment crossed his face, because Jean-Pierre did not remember getting undressed. The time laps concerned him, nevertheless, his desire for her pushed those thoughts aside. But when he opened his mouth to speak, Domonique placed her finger across his lips and silenced him. "Shh, don't talk, don't think, just feel." She whispered.

Jean-Pierre wanted to say what he was going to say before the perfume finger touched his lips. He wanted to say 'don't forget the condom.' But those words never came out. He proceeded without caution, without inhibition, and surrendered to the eroticism of Domonique's exotic beauty. He laid still for a while doing as he was told – not speaking, not thinking, just feeling. Feeling her lips around his penis and feeling endowed as it filled her mouth. Domonique sucked him hungrily, even when she gagged, she did not relent. At the height of their passion,

Jean-Pierre caved to the basic instinct of male dominance. He held Domonique's head as the thrust his hips upwards, causing her to nearly regurgitate her lunch. Next he maneuvered her on hands and knees and mounted her as a stallion would a mare. Domonique felt his power as he repeatedly rammed into her. She accepted him without resistance. Her shrilling voice resonated through the room from the combination of pleasure and pain. In an effort to concentrate, Domonique gripped the sheets as she contracted the muscles in her vaginal walls. Focusing on the intention to increase the friction for Jean-Pierre's quick release.

Not even a full minute had passed before Domonique felt the result of her technique. Jean-Pierre's breathing became rapid. The force of his body caused Domonique to lay flat on her belly, sandwiching her between the bed and himself. Jean-Pierre then released the guttural sound borne of pleasure and disappointment. For a moment he felt like a teenage boy who had absolutely no control of his libido, he was vex that his ejaculation was too soon. He laid still on top of Domonique absorbed in the barrage of emotions.

"Mmm" Domonique sounded, breaking the silence. "You have worn me out, I though you would never stop."

Her words suggested that his passion was long lasting. Her words, those very words placed a spell of confusion on Jean-Pierre. He did not know if he was inadequate or virile. How could she say 'I wore her out' he thought. Reflecting on the lunch, he thought maybe he drank too much wine, it could have clouded his judgment. He rolled off of her and concluded his thoughts 'well if she said I wore her out, I will not argue with that'.

Domonique reached for Jean-Pierre member and caressed it gently. Looking at him, she observed his closed eyes and a slight smile on his face. 'Yes' – she thought to herself, he's in a happy place right now, I put him there, he's mine.

Not counting the minutes that passed, Domonique felt the gradual increase in her palm. He touch seemed to be like magic as the flaccid member she caressed was resurrected once again.

Domonique steadily climbed onto Jean-Pierre, and his eyes opened when he felt the change from warm fingers to an incredibly hot, wet vagina.

"I thought you wanted to rest" he said.

"Quel genre d'hôte que je serais si je vous ai laissé voulant" (What kind of host would I be if I left you wanting?) she responded in French. Her mouth drew closer to his, kissing his lips, then his neck. Her kiss turned into a suck like a vampire, but without drawn blood. Jean-Pierre closed his eyes again, taken by the sensation. He felt the pulsing of his external jugular in her mouth, along with the sting from her thirsty lips. But the stinging feeling faded, replaced by the euphoric pleasure of Domonique's rocking body. Pelvis to pelvis she moaned, accepting all of him as she gave a mystical joyride.

Twenty five minutes later, that time has come again, Jean-Pierre's body could not conceal his overwhelming urge to climax. He held Domonique's hips, but he was not the one in control. She rode him more vigorously, and as she felt the first pulse from his penis – "donne le moi" (give it to me) she said. Then after he was spent, she said it again – "oui-oui donne le moi." (Yes-yes, give it to me.)

'I will drain you', Domonique thought to herself as she looked down on Jean-Pierre. Both smiling at each other, but for two completely different reasons. Him – because he's intoxicated with her beauty and lust. Her – because his sperm are swimming inside of her and she's looking at the telltale hickey that Sharon has to see when he goes home.

Chapter 7

4:00 – PM

THE HOUSE WAS quiet since Kathrine's departure two hours ago. Janine was fastened to the couch with her eyes glued to the pages. Pages, that took her somewhere in the Atlantic on a honeymoon cruise. She was at the pool side of the upper deck taking in some sun and having strong hands massaging some sunscreen all over her body.

The sound of a Porsche 911 Carrera revving before the engine switched off, stopped the hands from continuing their caress. It also stopped the smell of the ocean breeze and postponed the honeymoon cruise in the Atlantic. Back to her reality, Jeanine secured the bookmark between the pages before placing the book on the coffee table.

As Patrick walked in, he greeted her with his usual "honey I'm home." Then he sat next to her.

"I see that you're taking full advantage of your perks." Said Jeanine, pausing just for a second then continued with - "going in late, leaving early, what's next?"

"How about a drive to the Palisades Mall and then dinner?"

Jeanine smiled – "We haven't been there in a while, such a tough choice."

Patrick brought his brows together to have that puzzled look on his face as he asked – "What's a tough choice?"

Jeanine then rambled off a list of restaurants which were in the fore of her mind.

"I.H.O.P, Outback Steakhouse, Crab Shack, Chili's, T.G.I Fraday's…"

The realization hit him and Patrick burst out with laughter. "Don't worry." He said while laughing, "We can buy from all of them if you like."

Jeanine didn't eat out much. She actually prefer to eat in the comfort of her home. But every now and again she finds excitement in the highly advertised franchised restaurants.

Ana walked in to inform Jeanine that she's prepping for class.

"Excuse, good afternoon Mr. Isaac"

"Good afternoon Ana" he said with that – I'm pleased to see you – tone in his voice. And for an instant he thought she would make a good match for Jean-Pierre if he was not already so deeply involved. But that thought went out as quickly as it came in, he was not about to play match-maker.

Ana focused her eyes on Jeanine. "Do you need anything? I leaving soon to class."

Jeanine did not bother to correct her, she believe that Ana will eventually get it. "No it's ok, but why so early? Did they change the schedule?"

"No, but I taking the bus today. I try call he, but he no answer he phone."

Jeanine was unsettled with this news. It's not like Jean-Pierre to abandon Ana. He promised to escort her to and from class until she can read and understand English well enough to get around safely on her own.

"Never mind the bus, Patrick and I are going out so we'll drop you to class."

Ana's eyes were full of joy and her smile was 'thank you' enough. She nodded politely and stepped backward out of the room.

*****

6:00 – PM

After saying good night to Marsha and Angeline, the two sales clerks, Andrew Bridges lock the door and flipped the sign from Open to Close. Just as he was walking away there was a tap on the glass. Immediately he thought it was a late customer so he turned to say – we're closed – but couldn't. Instead, he hurried back to the door and opened it.

"Glad I caught you Andrew, I left my keys and my phone in the office." Jean-Pierre said as he moved with quickened steps.

"Oh sir"

Jean-Pierre paused, giving Andrew his attention.

"Dr. Henderson was here and she left some shopping bags for you to take home."

"Okay thanks"

In his office, Jean-Pierre pressed the lid of what appears to be a music box. It opened slowly as if with hydraulics. Reaching in, he took his keys and phone then checked the list of missed calls and messages. Subsequently, he left a voice message apologizing to Ana and promised to pick her up from class. His eyes locked on the shopping bags and that feeling call guilt, snuck right in. He took a deep breath then exhaled as if to blow out the feeling. But it did not work, so he picked up the bags and left.

Andrew saw his boss coming with his hands full, so he went and held the door for him.

"Thank you Andrew, see you in the morning."

"Goodnight sir" Andrew said, noticing the gloom in his boss's voice.

After locking the door, Andrew continued to do his routine close of the day, by separating the float from the cash and P.O.S transactions. As usual he balanced and secured the bag in the office's safe for Jean-Pierre to make the deposit in the morning.

Alarm – check, cameras – check, doors – check, all secure. Just out of habit, as Andrew walks home, he double checks his actions to make sure that if any breach is made, it will be no fault of his.

*****

Andrew Bridges lived alone in a small one bedroom apartment. A simple mind's first impression of him is nerd or geek. For that, he was a bully magnet in school. Unfortunately it didn't end there.

After high school he enlisted in the army, thinking that it would be the end of his bullying. He went in with the 'all for one, one for all' mentality, a brotherhood with an unbreakable bond, on or off the battle field. Sadly, not all of the recruits felt the same.

Andrew did not have animosity for the drill sergeant. He looked at his bully tactics differently. He felt the instructor was doing his job to motivate them and get them mentally and physically tough. Unlike Bill and Eddie, who Andrew refer to in his mind as Jack and Ass. They always seem to go out of their way to prank him. When other recruits would tell them – "Take it easy with Bridges" Jack and Ass would push harder.

After six months, instead of accepting Andrew as a team member, Jack and Ass continued the abuse. What they did not know was Andrew had enough and the next one will be made an example.

Within twenty four hours after he made up his mind, Andrew came out of the shower to discover his uniform missing from his bunk. As he looked around the barracks, he noticed Jack and Ass snickering in a corner and looking in his direction, then simultaneously giving him the finger. He didn't need any more confirmation than that.

Andrew started moving towards them. For every step he took, his confidence increased. As he got closer he removed the towel from around his waist and let it slip from his fingers to the floor – exposing all of his pale skin. He didn't know quite why he did that, perhaps it was to signify the birth of the new him – so naked he enters the world. Or, perhaps it was to show that he too have balls. His testicles swung with each step. His body lean from the months of training and at that moment his confidence peaked to invincible.

When Andrew confronted the two men, one word came out of his mouth and it sounded more like a battle cry. It was a long drawn-out "whyyyy" synchronous with two punches, each connected with pin point accuracy to each man's chin. It could have been the combination of Andrew's force and their shock of the event that rendered them unconscious. Nevertheless, the requital didn't end there. Andrew then kneeled over the men one at a time, breaking and gnawing at the middle fingers they showed him, severing them from their base knuckles.

Andrew Bridges sat crossed-legged, grinning with blood in and around his mouth, and a finger in each hand. He was rocking back and forth while mumbling something. A fellow private stood by but not too close, was able to make out what was being repeated –

"Who ya gonna flip the bird to now?"

"Who ya gonna flip the bird to now?"

"Who ya gonna flip the bird to now?"

Andrew Bridges woke up in the disciplinary barracks with no recollection of how he got there. He stayed there for thirty days. During that time he saw the army's clinician three times per week. At the end of his thirty days, the doctor recommended that no charges should be brought against him because his paroxysm was stemmed from months of provocation. And furthermore, the subject has no recollection of the ordeal. He was then medically discharged for mental health issues.

Since Andrew could not be all that he can be in the army, he took a business management course. After that, he graduated from a technical training institute and bounced around as a temp until he landed a permanent position at Tech World.

Andrew doesn't think of the army any more than he thinks of Bill and Eddie – the Jack and Ass. They're not a topic that he discusses at any time. Although they did have a role to play in unlocking the extreme ways that he sometimes behave.

Chapter 8

7:00 – PM

J EAN-PIERRE FINALLY REACHED home. As he put the bags down
he saw Sharon on the sofa.

"Well hello, I see you started the party without me." He said
as he noticed two empty pizza boxes, the end part of a hot dog,
remnants of french-fries, and she was eating a quart of chocolate
ice cream. Real ice cream, not the brand that doesn't melt even if
it's left out of the fridge for days.

"You weren't invited." She said colder than the ice cream she
was eating.

"Ouch! What did I do to deserve that?"

Sharon looked at him crossly – paused for a second then
said – "You do not want me to answer that." Then she stuffed
another spoon of ice cream in her mouth.

Jean-Pierre didn't want to know what Sharon was mad about
and he didn't want to fight. There's no way she could've known
what he did so maybe it's just mood swings from hormonal
changes. So he thought, and decided to change the subject.

"So darling, clearly you're not hungry so I'm going to grab a shower then fix myself something to eat."

Sharon pretended not to hear him. She picked up the remote and turned the television volume up, totally dismissing his presence. She promised herself that she will not shed another tear. She cried enough today, "No more tears" she whispered to herself after he vanished to the bathroom. It took every fiber of her being not to comment on what she saw on his neck.

Jean-Pierre stood under the shower, letting the water beat on his head. Perhaps he thought it would wash away the guilt. It didn't, so he resorted to justifying his behavior with an ideology that he doesn't truly believe in. Out of the shower the battle with himself continued. Wrapped in a towel he stood before the vanity, bracing himself with his arms.as he stares in the mirror at a very obvious hickey on his neck. As he surrendered to that belief, the image looking back at him said – "just sowing wild oats."

Jean-Pierre got dressed quickly. Blue jeans, black Taka high-neck Latin shirt and black leather riding vest. When he entered the living room he sat next to Sharon and rubbed her abdomen. She did not reject him even though she wanted to. Because feeling the baby move when he touched her, made her realize that he already made a connection. And breaking it is not something she wants to do.

Sharon was very keen. She muted the television and asked – "Where are you going?" in a voice not as grouchy as before.

"I'm going for a bite, then I'm going to H.L.I"

"Oh, you're going for Ana."

"Yes, do you need me to bring back something?"

"Just yourself, make sure you come home." Then she deliberately caressed the side of his neck where she saw the hickey and delivered a subtle blow with her words. "Don't let the vampire get you again." She whispered, then turned her face to the television and unmute it.

Jean-Pierre accepted the hint. Without saying another word he got up and went for his helmet, then he left. He knew that she must have seen the hickey when he came home. He also knew that she did not want an excuse or an explanation. So when guilt came back and defeated ideology, he offered none.

*****

7:45 – PM

George Polovski, an American born from an American mother and Russian father. At forty three he was the proud owner of Great Seafood Bar & Restaurant. For his grand opening he had the television news crew along with other media outlets to share his historical grand opening announcement. 'happy hour – buy one get the other free at the bar, and in the restaurant, the first fifty patrons will get free vodka with their meals, every time, not just on the day of the grand opening.' He also had a simple slogan, and it worked. "Great Seafood – our name speaks for itself."

George usually doesn't get home this early, but Kathrine called and it sounded urgent.

"Kathrine" he called out but there was no answer.

"Natalya" he called, and still no answer. George made his way from room to room on the main floor. There was no sign of disturbance, but for his own comfort he drew his firearm and stealthily went up the stairs. At the top of the stairs, George saw flicker of lights emitting from his room. He quickened his pace, thinking its fire, but wait – there was no smoke.

When George arrived at his room, he stood in the doorway in awe. His wife sat on the bed in a red Fredrick's of Hollywood lingerie and the room was adorned with about a hundred strawberry scented candles.

George slid the safety and holstered his weapon, then released a sigh of relief.

"You had me worried." He said.

Kathrine stood up to face him, did a three hundred and sixty degrees turn and stopped with her arms akimbo. "Do you like?" She asked. But George simply nodded, he couldn't wipe the grin off his face. It was the kind of grin that a kid would have if he was told he can have all the candy in the store, but everything so desirable that he didn't know where to begin. But George didn't have to make up his mind, Kathrine did it for him. She went and closed the door then undressed him. After, she led him to the bed and sat him down at its edge. She knelt in front of him, held his penis in her hand as she gazed into his eyes and said "I want us to feel like newlyweds again. I want the sparks to fly when we touch."

George's already hard penis seemed to take on a life of its own as it twitched with anticipation in her palm. Kathrine didn't let him suffer for long, she filled her mouth with him. After approximately ten minutes of fellatio, she rose up and spoke softly to him – "Your turn to undress me."

"With pleasure" he responded, then gently began to remove her lingerie.

There was an object on the bed and Kathrine picked it up then laid flat on her back with her arm extended to her husband. "I bought this with the lingerie today."

"Mmm, interesting" he said as he took the vibrator from her. It had an oval shape tip and a handle like a toothbrush. Kathrine was sure to purchase something that wouldn't intimidate George. The dildo vibrator combination that she had her eyes on, would have made him feel inept.

George skillfully executed cunnilingus while using the vibrator on Kathrine's clitoris. She moaned, sounds escaped her mouth that George never heard before. Her body jerked, her hips rose and fell as if possessed. Her pulsing vagina gripped his tongue as if trying to have him go deeper. Her body quivered and then it happened, – a long scream signified her overwhelming ecstatic orgasm which came in a fury of three successions.

George was on a high, the squirts in his face triggered the animal in him. His wife never squirted during an orgasm before, so this took them both to new heights. He licked her inner thighs and inhaled deeply, taking in the scent of the woman he loved so dearly. He raised up to kiss her nipples and simultaneously inserted himself. The moans and groans were from joy not pain, and an indicator of the revival of their passion. The grinding did not stop. Then Kathrine was feeling the rush upon her again, that 'in the sky', 'head in the clouds' feeling. And just as her voice was getting louder with – "Yes! Yes! Yes! Oh God yes." George slammed harder and harder to bring them both to the finish line – at the same time. The sweet scent of strawberries filled the air and the sweat of their bodies shimmered under the candle lights.

Kathrine looked up into the ceiling then into his eyes.

"I'm sorry" she said

"For what?" he asked with a puzzled look on his face.

"For holding back and keeping you out of my troubled thoughts. You're my husband and I should've communicated better."

"It's okay, I guess I should've asked if there was something wrong. I didn't make a big deal out of it."

"Well it is a big deal, I don't want my lack of affection to send you in someone else's arms." She said with an almost whining tone.

"Is that what you've been thinking?"

Kathrine just nodded in the affirmative. And George said exactly what she wanted to hear. – "Your arms are the only arms I want to be in." Then he kissed her gently.

After the kiss, Kathrine asked – "Do you remember when we were newlyweds you wanted to try something new to me, and I said I wasn't into that and you never asked again?"

"Uh-huh"

"Well I want you to do it, whatever fantasies you have, I want you to live them with me. I want to be your every desire." Not giving him a chance to respond she reached under the pillow, retrieved a tube of lubricant and handed it to him.

George had a look of utter disbelief on his face.

"I picked that up with the lingerie too."

"You don't have to do this" said George

Kathrine sat up and with firmness to her voice she said – "In the restaurant you hire the best chef, the best bartender, the most polite waitresses, why?"

George just stared at her so she asked again – "Why?"

This time he answered – "To please the customers."

"And why would you want to please the customers?"

The answer was obvious but George obliged her with it. "So they will come again."

"Because if you didn't put things in place to make the customer's experience a great one, what can ultimately happen?"

And again he obliged her – "They can dine elsewhere."

"Exactly!" she said then continued – "I want to be your first-class restaurant, and I don't want you dining anywhere but here." As she said that, she balled up a fist and extended her index finger pointing to herself. "This restaurant is always open to you. You can choose any dish on its menu." Kathrine then rolled on her stomach, pulled her knees under and raised her bottom in the air.

George's head spun with excitement. He went to the vodka rack in his room and grabbed a Bacardi, then he placed it back. His hand touched the Grey Goose, then the Smirnoff, but he decided to settle with the Absolut, because at that moment his wife's peach shaped ass looked absolutely beautiful. He poured himself a double and drank it in one gulp.

George then opened the tube and squeezed some lubricant in his palm. He approached his wife's peach and kissed both sides. The kid in the candy store grin reappeared, he was about to try another flavor. As he inserted a lubricated finger in Kathrine's tight peach hole, one line of Phil Collins's 'In The Air Tonight' played in his head – "I've been waiting for this moment, for all my life – oh Lord". He doesn't know why it jumped into his head, maybe it befitted his emotions.

George then lubed himself and entered her virgin peach slowly. She moaned as he stroked her gently. He felt her sphincter grip his shaft, then he increased the rhythm of his stroke.

He paused for a moment to roll on his side and reached for their new toy. He gave it to her to use and she touched where it was most effective. George felt the rapid pulsing of her sphincter and Kathrine's orgasm came in a rush, bringing with it some urine. He rolled with her, not disconnecting from his sweet peach. She was faced down and they locked fingers over her head. She arched her back, giving him access to all of her peach. She fed him and fed him, until he was full. George released a sigh of satisfaction then laid cuddling in their sweat.

"You okay hun?" George asked

"Wonderful, it wasn't as painful as I imagined." But she left out that he and the vibrator make a superb team. She can't remember ever climaxing so many times in a session.

Kathrine however, did not have to hide those thoughts. George was okay with the new addition to their bedroom, because it helped to achieve a mutual desire. He was not too macho to accept it.

"Come on hun, let's take a shower and get out of here."

"Where to?" Kathrine asked.

"Back to the restaurant."

"Ugh, how about you let the man you left in charge when you're not there, do his job and we can shower and come back to bed."

"Sounds good hun, but you know I like to count my own money."

With that said, they showered and Kathrine stayed home while George went to Great Seafood Bar & Restaurant.

Chapter 9

8:30 – PM

A NA EXITED THE building of H.L.I and smiled when she saw Jean-Pierre. She said goodbye to her Mexican classmate who was walking with her. The woman held Ana's arm quickly and asked – "Es ese tu novio" (Is that your boyfriend?) Ana was going to say 'just friends' but thought carefully and said "mi familia" (my family). The woman smiled then asked – "Puede presentarme" (can you introduce me?)

"Ahora no, la proximavez" (not now, next time.) They parted ways and Ana went to Jean-Pierre.

"Good evening" Ana said

"Good evening" he responded, in a tone Ana is not accustomed to then handed her his helmet.

"Are you okay?" She asked, seeing that he was not his jovial self when he's around her.

Jean-Pierre just nodded then puts on his Global Vision riding glasses.

"Ready?" he asked in that same monotone.

And as she indicated yes, it was ignition – throttle – gone.

*****

8:50 – PM

A ride that was supposed to take approximately thirty minutes, took fifteen. Ana dismounted, gave Jean-Pierre his helmet then went inside crying. Jean-Pierre went after her.

"Ana I'm sorry" he shouted. And in her broken English she shouted back in hysteria "If you no want come for me, telly me, no try killy me."

"No that's not it, it's... never mind" he said, with sadness trailing his words.

Ana observed his slumped posture and a look of dejection in his eyes, then her anger turned to concern for him. "Qué pasa" (What's wrong?) she asked.

"No te preocupes, es mi problema" (don't worry, it's my problem) he said, too ashamed to tell her he behaved like a callous cad. Then he took a slow walk to the kitchen.

"Would you like some coffee?" he asked.

"Yes, thank you."

As he was making the coffee it dawned on him that his parents were not home.

"Where are my parents?" he asked, but not worried, just curious.

"They went to the mall" Ana said, pleased with herself for answering with clarity.

Jean-Pierre offered Ana a cup, then he held his cup out and apologized again. She accepted and touched cups before she sipped.

Jean-Pierre finished his coffee in silence, then hugged Ana before he left.

*****

10:15 – PM

In the elevator, Jean-Pierre reflected on his cruising speed going home on I-495w. If he was traveling any faster, he could've been in the collision ahead of him.

The elevator door opened and broke his thought. Jean-Pierre then took a slow walk to his apartment. He was not in any hurry to face Sharon.

When he stepped in he did not see her on the couch. The area was cleaned from any signs of feasting. So he proceeded to the bedroom where the crescent moon lending its light through the window, presented her silhouette.

She was fast asleep and he did not want to wake her. He undressed quickly then quietly went to bed. However, Sharon did feel him but did not turn to face him. Therefore Jean-Pierre felt he was successful in sneaking to bed, and watched the ceiling till he fell asleep.

Chapter 10

12 – Midnight

DOMONIQUE SALISBURY DONNED in a ritual hooded cloak, lit eleven candles – ten white and one red. Then she placed a black string, thirteen inches in length in front of the red candle. She chanted something in a whisper, an almost inaudible prayer.

She then wrapped the string around the red candle several times before tying it into a knot. Continuing with her chant she became more vocal, speaking slowly and clearly.

"A sacrifice to you, take what is thine. A sacrifice to you, leave me with mine."

Domonique repeated this thirty three times. After which, only the white candles remained. The red candle melted over the black string, then both candle and string vanished.

She stood with her eyes looking menacing under the hood. Then she said loud enough for herself to hear – "Yesss" dragging the S at the end of the word. "It is time to take back what is rightfully mine."

*****

1:00 – AM

Jeanine tossed in her sleep, the dream of her son drowning, wanting to breath but cannot. It jolted her awake with outstretched arms reaching to pull him up and a frightening cry "mon fils" (my son) that woke her husband.

Patrick embraced her – "It's alright, you just had a nightmare."

"No, it felt too real to be just a dream." She said, as she allowed him to persuade her to lay back down. But her unfettered mind travelled while her body stayed in the boundaries of his arms.

*****

5:45 – AM

Kathrine was already at the Isaac's home waiting on Jeanine for them to go on their morning walk. Just as the door opened, Jeanine said – "you're quite early"

"I could hardly wait to talk to you." Said Kathrine

"What's the matter?" Jeanine asked looking very concerned.

"Oh nothing's the matter, I'm just anxious to share the good news. But first, let's warm up and be on our way."

As she bent down to stretch, she asked "Didn't you say that Patrick would join us today?"

"I said that's what he said, and he said it again when he saw me getting ready. And I quote 'I didn't forget baby, I'll join you tomorrow'." Jeanine and Kathrine laughed as they continued to stretch.

After the walk began, Jeanine seemed to be the anxious one. "Well?" she probed.

With a smile Kathrine said "I will not get into details because it's not lady-like. But I will say, the tiger roamed all of his jungle last night and I thoroughly enjoyed it. So, thank you for your advice yesterday."

Feeling happy for her friend, Jeanine said – "You're welcome, now let's pick up the pace."

They did just that, and caught up to some other early birds who were equally committed to their morning exercises.

*****

7:00 – AM

The weather was nice in Manhattan but Jean-Pierre opted to stay indoors. Instead of going to central park, he switched on his treadmill and set it on incline for two miles.

After his run he realized that Sharon did not wake up, but decided to wake her after his shower. In the shower he made another decision. One that he knew would change his life. He decided to buy a ring and ask Sharon to marry him. He hoped that the proposal will show her that he chose to commit, a sign of the end of affairs.

Out of the shower the mirror reminded him of his indiscretion. The hickey that told the story was still talking to him. And to shut it up, he got dress quickly.

Jean-Pierre sat on the bed next to Sharon. "Beautiful" he whispered to her "wake up".

"Mmm, not ready" Sharon protested in a low tone.

He noticed her skin appeared clammy, so he touched her forehead with the back of his hand. "You feel a bit warmer than usual, are you okay?"

Sharon gave a half smile, looked up with drowsy eyes and said "Thanks for your concern, but it's just hot-flashes."

"Okay then, I'm going to the office early, do you need me to fix something for you to eat."

"It's ok, have a good day"

Jean-Pierre kissed her cheeks then left. He did not feel that bond, he felt a coldness instead. He knew that she must still be upset, but he also knew how he planned to win her back.

*****

8:30 – AM

Andrew Bridges arrived at Tech World to meet the galvanize shutters already rolled up. He unlocked, entered and relocked the door. Making his way to the office he took a mental note of a task that needs to be done – 'the glass display counter needs to be cleaned of customers smudged hand prints'.

The door was wide open so he needn't knock. "Good morning boss" he said as he walked in.

"Good morning Andrew, how are you?"

"Okay, and you?"

"Just wonderful, I went over the books this morning and all is well. Next, we're getting a delivery today of the new cellular phones."

Jean-Pierre passed him a folder and continued the briefing.

"The varied selling prices are in there. I'm leaving to go to the bank for 10:00, just in case I don't return on time, I'm expecting the young man from yesterday."

Andrew raised an eyebrow but said nothing. Jean-Pierre continued to speak.

"His name is Johnny Santiago. He's a student at Park West High School. I want to mentor him, if you want to chip in, that would be a good thing."

Andrew just listened and did not respond, so Jean-Pierre continued.

"I told Johnny that his first week is paying restitution, after that he would be employed part-time, giving him something positive to do after school. So just in case he sticks to his word and show up, show him around and keep him busy."

"You got it boss."

Both Andrew and Jean-Pierre took notice of the time. Jean-Pierre passed the float to Andrew, then Andrew left to set up the cash register.

Right after he was finished there was a knock on the door, it was Angeline. He lets her in and left the door unlocked, then flipped the sign from Close to Open.

Marsha strolled in five minutes later with the end of a bagel in one hand and a half cup of coffee in the other. "Sorry I'm late Andrew, the line at Starbucks was crazy this morning."

"Is it ever sane?" he responded. But she looked at him weird, not use to him be anything but serious.

"It's a joke" he said unmuting the silence. Then Angeline laughed, and Andrew gave her an appreciative smile before continuing with his duties.

*****

10:30 – AM

The telephone rang at the Isaac's home in University Gardens. After answering, Ana ran to Jeanine, "emergency" she said as she handed her the phone.

"Hello, Mrs. Isaac speaking."

"Good morning Mrs. Isaac, my name is Dr. Chapman. I'm calling from New York Presbyterian Hospital on behalf of Dr. Sharon Henderson. We're trying to reach the father of her baby."

"What's wrong?" Jeanine asked with unmistakable worry in her voice.

"I'm not at liberty to say, but what I will tell you – she has been admitted and she's under observation."

"Thank you doctor." Jeanine said.

Jeanine called Tech World after she was unsuccessful in reaching Jean-Pierre on his cell phone.

"Tech World, Andrew speaking, how may I help you?" Andrew answered in a very pleasant 'we care about you' voice.

"Good morning Andrew this is Mrs. Isaac, is my son in?"

"I'm afraid not, is there something I could do?" He asked out of courtesy, knowing very well the call was personal and not business. So her answer surprised him.

"Yes, if you get in touch with him, please tell him to meet me at the New York Presbyterian Hospital, it's urgent."

"Um which one?"

"The one in midtown."

"OK as soon as I touch base I'll let him know."

"Thank you." She said then quickly hung up. She was about to call Patrick but remembered he said that he had an important meeting, so instead, she called a taxi service and left the information with Ana to be passed on.

*****

10:30 – AM

Jean-Pierre was eleven minutes away by foot from New York Presbyterian Hospital. He stood inside of Lauren B Fine Jewelry and Diamonds, looking over the engagement rings. His phone was never switched back on after his meeting in the bank. Therefore, he was oblivious to all the emergency calls about the woman he loves, laying in a hospital bed just minutes away from him.

He pointed to a stunning piece. "I would like to see that one please." He said to the blond sales clerk with a suspicious eye, who looked at him keenly. Then with the audacity said "Sir perhaps you did not see the other zero. It's not five thousand, it's fifty thousand."

Jean-Pierre was about to respond to the obvious racial profiling but chose to play a game with her instead.

"Oh my, you're right, thank you." He said.

The clerk smiled and nodded, mentally giving herself a good-job pat on the shoulder for making the right assessment of who she thought of as a blue collar worker. Then to her amazement she heard.

"My girlfriend would've thought I was cheap to propose with that. I thought it said five hundred thousand, thank you for pointing out that it's only fifty thousand. Now please show me a piece worthy for the bride to be."

"You're joking right?" She asked, looking embarrassed

"Yes, but I do want to see this ring for fifty thousand."

After examining the ring he asked – "What size is this?"

"It's a six"

"Then it's perfect, I need it in a red case please."

"And how will you be paying sir?"

Jean-Pierre took out his Amex platinum card along with his driver's license and passed them to her. After she inspected them, she asked – "Would you like the ring insured Mr. Isaac?"

"I have my own agent, thank you."

After processing the sale, the clerk returned his credentials and offered somewhat of an apology – "It wasn't my intention to insult or embarrass you concerning the cost of the ring, so I hope you did not feel neither."

"My advice to you, remember that you're in the business of service. If you rub a customer the wrong way, you could very well miss out on an important sale. Only because I'm a friend of your boss I did business here today. Tell him Mr. Isaac said hi and I'll see him on the golf course." Then he winked at her and left her standing with her mouth agape.

*****

11:15 – AM

Jean-Pierre returned to Tech World. Just as he was about to speak, Andrew cut him off. "Boss I've been trying to reach you. Your mother called and said you need to meet her at New York Presbyterian Hospital ASAP."

Jean-Pierre looked at his phone, switched it on then asked – "what happened?" in a voice that was noticeably shaky.

"I don't know, she didn't say. She just said to give you the message, oh, it's the one in midtown."

Jean-Pierre said a quick thank you, then he was gone.

Fifteen minutes later, the taxi Jean-Pierre was in, encountered traffic jam.

"I'll get out here, this looks like it'll take another twenty five minutes. I can run the distance in three." He paid the cabbie and started to run.

True to his estimate, Jean-Pierre arrived at the hospital in three minutes. He went straight to the information center, breathing heavy with an obvious elevated heart rate. Before he could enquire, a nurse asked "Sir are you okay? May I help you?"

"Yes, my name is Jean-Pierre Isaac, I received a message from…" He was interrupted by an admin staff behind the counter.

"Mr. Isaac"

"Yes" he answered, then motioned towards the admin staff with the name tag S. Cox. She handed him a visitor's badge and pointed to an x on the clipboard for him to sign in. "We were expecting you. Your mother is with her on the 7th floor, room 711."

"Thank you"

Taking quick strides to the elevator, the words played back in his head – 'your mother is with her on the 7th floor'. Then his eyes focused on the direction chart next to the elevator. They saw only the 7th floor, which read 'Antepartum Unit'. Then the realization hit him.

"Sharon" he said out loud, not minding the people around him. He pressed the button again and again as if that will make the door close faster, it didn't.

*****

11:38 – AM

Inside room 711, Jean-Pierre hugged his mother with relief that she was well. Then he turned his attention to Sharon and held her hand. She was hooked up to various monitors which read hers and the fetus's vitals.

"I guess it wasn't just hot flashes. I'm sorry, I shouldn't have left you." He said.

Sharon sounded weak, she spoke in a very low voice – "It's not your fault."

Jean-Pierre went down on one knee and pulled the red velvet case from his pocket. He removed his shades, looked into Sharon's eyes and spoke.

"I know this might not be the best timing, but there's no time like the present. And I know that I have caused your heart to ache, but I promise you Sharon, from this day onwards I will do everything in my power to bring you joy." Then opened the case and showed her the ring. "Will you marry me?"

Jeanine put one hand over her heart and sighed with a teary-eyed happiness even though he didn't discuss it with her.

Sharon smiled and barely lifted her left hand as she mouthed the word "Yes". And as the ring was placed on her finger, tears ran down her cheeks. Jean-Pierre kissed her hand and she went to sleep.

A few minutes later the doctor walked in.

"Mr. Isaac"

"Yes doctor"

"We're running some test, so far we're not sure what caused the rise in temperature."

"What about our baby"

"I was getting to that." The doctor paused, then chose his words carefully. "I have to run some test. The fetal monitor is showing some abnormal and conflicting readings."

"What do you mean?" Jean-Pierre asked as Jeanine stood quietly listening to every word and became deeply concerned. She feared the dream she had last night was not Jean-Pierre, but his unborn child.

The doctor continued to explain – "At first the monitor showed one fetus then later it showed two, then it showed one again."

"Maybe your machine is faulty." Jean-Pierre expressed to the doctor.

"Maybe, maybe not. For now please her rest, I'll keep you informed."

Chapter 11

12:30 – PM

GEORGE AND KATHRINE finished their meals, each with a glass of wine. It was George's first meal of the day. He usually sleeps late since the restaurant opens from 4PM to midnight, and he doesn't reach home until about 1:30 in the morning.

Natalya began to clear the table and asked "Would any of you like something else?"

Kathrine answered "No that'll be all, thank you."

Then George said "Just a minute, what's the name of that sauce you put on the fish"

"It's a Hungarian sauce" Natalya answered proudly.

"I like it, maybe you should be working in the restaurant."

Kathrine gave a quick look at George but Natalya pick it up and answered.

"No no no, I'm just a home cook."

"Well I hope you wouldn't mind sharing it with my chef."

"Of course not, it is yours when you want it."

Kathrine jumped in, she thought Natalya's words were too close to her own from what she told George last night. "George I'll be coming for dinner tonight."

"Oh ok, are you riding with me?"

"No honey, you know I can't stay out so late. I have my morning exercise to do and that, I'm not trading."

Natalya interrupted and Kathrine did not look pleased.

"Kathrine I hope I'm not imposing, but if you like, I can come to the restaurant with you to show the chef the recipe, then keep you company on the drive back."

Kathrine was about to tell her it wasn't necessary but George spoke first.

"Great idea." He said. And that was that.

*****

Just down the road at the Isaac's residence the telephone rang.

"Hello"

"Hi Ana, let me speak to Jeanine please."

"Oh Mr. Isaac she is not here. She told me to tell you she is at hospital with Sharon. I have the information written down. If you hold on I can get it for you."

"No, that would not be necessary, thank you. I will call Jean-Pierre, see you when I get home."

"Okay bye, bye."

*****

2:00 – PM

Patrick entered room 711 "How is she?" he asked

"We don't know" his son answered somberly.

"Did any of you eat?"

Jeanine and her son shook their heads in the negative.

75

"Well not eating isn't going to help her, so let's go to the canteen and get something."

Jean-Pierre shook his head in the negative again, saying "I don't want to leave her."

His father put his hand on his shoulder "I understand, I'll be back."

"Pato, I'll come with you." Jeanine said, as Jean-Pierre helplessly looked on at his fiancée.

Twenty five minutes later his parents came back with food. Jeanine handed him a tray with fillet snapper with asparagus and baked potatoes.

After he ate, his mind came alive. Jean-Pierre called the limo service for them to chauffeur Ana, to and from class. He asked his mom to call Ana to give her an update, while he called the store.

"Good afternoon Tech World, Marsha speaking how may I help you?"

"Hi Marsha, I would like to speak to Andrew please."

Recognizing his voice Marsha responded – "Mr. Isaac, one moment please." Then signaled Andrew, who was talking to Johnny.

"Hello, Andrew speaking."

"Andrew, I will not be returning today."

"Boss, how is your mom?"

"My mom" Jean-Pierre realized that, like himself, Andrew thought it was his mother in the hospital.

"My mom is okay, its Sharon who is not well." He explained.

"Dr. Henderson, what happened?"

"We don't know yet Andrew, but I'm sure she'll be fine." Jean-Pierre said with confidence, but not feeling his own words.

"Oh, the kid is here Johnny."

"Good, take of things, we'll catch up later."

"Okay, goodbye sir." Andrew Bridges hung up the phone and felt a sudden sense of melancholy overshadowing him.

*****

3:30 – PM

Domonique Salisbury finally woke up, but still felt drowsy. She was completely drained after the ritual. Now she must eat, but she was too tired to go out. She found her way to the refrigerator, peered in, then filled with uncertainty, she closed it back. Eventually she reached in her fruit bowl on the kitchen counter and settled for a banana. After that was consumed, Domonique set her alarm for 11:45 PM and went back to bed. She clutched her pillow and thought of Jean-Pierre and the baby she would have for him. She took comfort in those thoughts until she fell asleep.

*****

5:00 – PM

Dr. Sharon Henderson was awake and enjoying the faces of who she now calls her family. Jean-Pierre, his mother and father all smiled back at her.

While she was still asleep, Jean-Pierre told his father of the proposal and acceptance.

Patrick was very proud and told him – "Son that is the honorable and manly thing to do, congratulations."

Now that Sharon is up and bright-eyed, Jeanine said "let's see how soon you can come home, this is not the place to celebrate an engagement."

"Yes I second the motion" JP said happily. Then the doctor walked in with his chart in hand.

"I have good news and bad news." All worried eyes were on him. Then he said "Dr. Henderson, all your test came back normal. The all released a notable sigh of relief.

Then Sharon asked "so what's the bad news?"

"The bad news is I'm not discharging you now. Just as a precaution, we're keeping you overnight for observation. If all goes well, then you'll be home for lunch tomorrow. Now, if you'll excuse me, I'm being paged." Like the wind, he was gone almost as quickly as he came.

"Mr. and Mrs. Isaac..." Sharon started, when cut short by Jeanine.

"Mom is fine, get used to it."

Sharon's exposed teeth were enough to show that she was pleased with the gesture. Then she continued "I really appreciate you two being her, but I don't want you driving back too late." Patrick responded to her concern –

"Now, now don't worry about it, your fiancé ..." He emphasized on the word fiancé and paused for the word to be absorbed by everyone. "...Took care of that while you slept. He figured it would be more convenient for us to stay at the penthouse. So we'll be 15 minutes away if you need us. But we'll leave you two to your privacy and we'll see you tomorrow." With that said, Jeanine went and kissed Sharon's forehead and gave her son a hug before they left.

When her future in-laws were gone Sharon expressed her fears to Jean-Pierre.

"JP I'm scared." He held her hand firmly to reassure her.

"I'm right here, I'm not going anywhere."

"Not that" she said, then resumed "The doctor said everything is normal, but it doesn't feel like it."

JP saw real fear in her eyes and felt helpless.

"One of the nurses who came in while you were asleep assured me that you're at the right place, because this hospital has one of the best prenatal unit in the city."

Sharon said okay just to appease him, seeing her fears mirroring in his eyes.

*****

8:00 – PM

On the way back from Great Seafood, Kathrine drove her mustang in silence. She was reevaluating her passenger's relationship with George. 'Maybe' she thought, 'maybe I am paranoid. Perhaps George was just being nice.'

Her private thoughts did not slacken her focus on the road. In her mirrors she saw a fast approaching vehicle in the lane to her left. Just as it cleared her, without indicating it switched lanes, cutting her off.

With perfect timing Kathrine downshifted and maneuvered into the lane from which the vehicle came.

Natalya screamed "Whoa" as she held firm on the grab-handle. Then she looked across at Kathrine to see her narrowed her eyes, pursed her lips and accelerated.

"What are you doing!?" Natalya shouted. Kathrine did not answer, she maintained pursuit of the white sedan that cut her off.

One mile later the driver of the sedan pulled off the road when he realized that he was being followed by the same car he had cut off, and Kathrine pulled right behind him.

As soon as he stepped out of his car, Kathrine dislodged the pepper spray connected to her car keys and stepped out to meet him. Natalya was scared, but the thought 'strength in numbers' popped into her head, so she unfastened her seat belt to get out. But it was too late, she was paralyzed but what she heard and saw.

"What ya following me for bitch?" the driver said aggressively while approaching Kathrine.

"You almost caused an accident asshole!" Kathrine yelled back.

"Ya better get back in ya car, cause ya can still have that accident."

Kathrine's right foot suddenly went up and connected with testicles. The man let out a scream as he bent forward in agony.

Then he heard "Who's the bitch now?" right before the burning sensation in his eyes.

Kathrine nonchalantly walked back to her car and peeled out when she passed him.

Twenty minutes later Kathrine pulled into her driveway. Before she exited, Natalya looked at Kathrine and said "You're amazing, you handle yourself and this car very well."

"Thank you" Kathrine said, then added "A woman got to know how to handle her stick" then pulled the handbrake hoping that Natalya got the double meaning. That she doesn't need help handling George.

Once inside, Natalya went to the kitchen and prepared two glasses of wine. When she returned to the living room Kathrine was already upstairs. Natalya trailed her to her room and called out. "Kathrine"

Kathrine opened the door and was pleasantly surprised to see Natalya with wine.

"I thought might want to wind down from all that excitement."

"Thank you Natalya, how thoughtful" Kathrine said, feeling genuinely pleased.

"Kathrine can I talk to you?"

"Sure" Kathrine answered, still standing by her door.

"Can we sit?" Natalya asked.

"Certainly, come in"

They walked to the couch and sat, then out of fear that Kathrine would drop her glass, Natalya took it and placed it with hers on the side table. This caused Kathrine to worry.

"I don't want you to judge me. I just want you to hear me out before you say anything, okay?

"Okay" Kathrine said anxiously, hoping this woman next to her isn't going to tell her she is sleeping... correction ... fucking her husband.

"I have a confession to make."

That's it, Kathrine thought, those words are the prelude of it all.

Natalya continued "I think you're beautiful, and I can't hold back these feeling that I have for you." Kathrine wondered if she was hearing correctly, but did not interrupt.

"This beautiful diamond you gave me made me want to express myself to you, but I was afraid. Then last night you told me to have the evening to myself and enjoy a movie. When I returned home, I heard you with your husband. I was very jealous, because I wanted to make you make those sounds."

"Stop, say no more, its wrong."

"You promised to hear me out and not judge."

"Look Natalya, I'm flattered, but I've always been repulsed by the thought of two vaginas rubbing. I want to feel insertion and not by a rubber dick. I have nothing against you if you want to be a lesbian, but I am not one."

"Neither am I." Natalya rebutted, then continued "I love the feeling of the penis inside of me too, but I also enjoy the company of a woman who is beautiful and sensual as yourself. Now let me finish. When I was changing your sheets, this morning, I found your toy and placed it back under your pillow. I imagined how wonderful it would be to use it with you."

"Okay, that enough." Kathrine said, attempting to stand up.

"Kathrine are you telling me you never imagined what it would be like? It never ever, crossed your mind, and only because of fear of some kind of backlash prevented you from experimenting? It's okay to lie to others if it's saving yourself, but when you lie to yourself the truth looks at you in the mirror."

Kathrine looked deep into her eyes and said "Natalya this isn't going to happen okay, and don't worry I'll keep this conversation just between us."

"Okay, can I at least get a friendship hug?"

Kathrine opened her arms for the embrace. When Natalya hugged her, she whispered "You were so brave tonight, it turned me on watching you kick that guy's ass." Then Natalya went brave one last time, she planted a passionate kiss on Kathrine's lips.

Kathrine did not move right away. Either from the shock of disbelief or the arousing tingle that snuck into her being while her guard was down. Natalya moved swiftly and aggressively. By the time she moved her lips from Kathrine's lips, she was kissing her neck.

Kathrine finally pushed her off. "Don't ever let that happen again."

Natalya smiled and said "Nothing can happen unless you want it to happen. I saw how you beat a man, so if you really wanted to stop me you could have."

Natalya picked up her glass of wine and headed for the door. She looked over her shoulder and said "You don't have to lie to yourself anymore."

Kathrine went to close the door. In her mind she protested and categorically denied the arousal she felt. In an attempt to wash away what she thought was filth, she rushed to the bathroom. When she undressed, her panty-liner revealed the truth. But still in a state of dubiety, she took her middle finger and ran it gently between her slit. The slippery substance she felt as she rubbed her thumb and middle finger together, confirmed her unfathomable desire.

Chapter 12

9:30 – PM

ANDREW BRIDGES FINISHED his burger and fries then washed them down with a vanilla shake. He exited the fast food joint and headed downtown on foot. He felt anxious, it has been a month since he last went for his therapy.

A few blocks later, the anxiety stirred something in his stomach. "Wow! Still hungry?" he said aloud, as if talking to a companion. Then about ten yards later he stopped at a hotdog stand and ordered a knish. After he was served, the vendor said –"That'll be $3.50"

"$3.50, since when?" Andrew asked surprisingly.

"Since the mayor appointed that new health commissioner, Dr. whatever his name is." The vendor answered, then continued to explain to his customer. "They changed the regulations on the temperature that is safe for certain foods. Therefore we had to upgrade our food carts to meet the new standards. The association agreed that it was understandable. After all, nobody wants a customer to get food poison. It'll be bad for business. But the real problem is this – they increased the cost of the permit. That's just plain extortion. So I hope you understand why the knish is $3.50."

Andrew then took a five dollar bill from his wallet and said "Thank you, keep the change."

"And thank you." Said the vendor.

He continued his walk while taking small bites of the potato knish until it was consumed. Andrew wiped his mouth and threw the napkin in the rubbish bin on the corner.

Suddenly, alerted by scurrying steps, he looked over his shoulder and braced himself for the expected assault. But it didn't come. There were two seemingly homeless men rushing to the bin to see what new treasures they can find.

Andrew relaxed a bit, but did not drop his guard. He was in the heart of Chinatown, on Mott Street. A place that could be considered peaceful or a real health hazard, depending on one's individual experience.

Finally he arrived at his destination, Lucky Stem Massage Therapy.

Inside he's greeted by a short, corpulent, middle age Asian woman with a typical Chinese bang hairstyle. "Welcome back" – and being familiar with his face, she asked "will you have your usual treatment or something less intense?"

"The usual"

"Right this way"

He followed her to a room where payments are made, then he was led to what's known as the executive suite. "Make yourself comfortable, you will be attended to momentarily." She said this with a perfect smile. A smile Andrew was sure that she practiced for many years.

As he waited, he looked around. He has been to other executive suites before, but it was his first time in the one which he stands. It seems like they all have a standard décor. This one however, was windowless and looks about 17-feet by 17-feet. In it was a massage table with a shelf below it containing an array of oils and lotions. Also, there was an eye catching frameless glass shower stall with double removable massage shower heads, and a queen size bed with a mini-bar next to it. Just as he nodded, affirming his visual appreciation, the door opened. Two beautiful Chinese women walked in, closed and locked the door behind them.

"Are you ready to be happy?" the round faced one asked.

"Very ready." Andrew replied.

Then both women disrobed, one was about 110 pounds and the other was her extreme opposite, weighing about 220 pounds. Exactly what he requested, someone petite and someone plump.

Andrew stood very relaxed as the women undressed him. His two hours of therapy has officially begun.

They walked him to the shower. It was large enough for all three to fit comfortably. The petite one removed one of the shower heads and before she turned it on she said –"I'm called Soot-Yew, because whatever suits you I will do."

Then the plump one selected a bath scrub, poured piña colada scented body wash on it then said "And I'm called Annie-Ting, because anything you want I will give."

Both women giggled and began to bathe him. They washed every part of him, from head to toes. The water was hot but not to burn him. Five minutes later Andrew felt sterilized stepping out of the steaming shower, with steam literally coming off his skin.

Soot-Yew and Annie-Ting dried him, then placed him faced down on the massage table. With Soot-Yew to his left and Annie-Ting to his right, they moisturized their hands and started on his feet, demonstrating their skills in reflexology.

They worked their hands until they reached his crown, then they turned him over and worked from the crown straight down.

Soot-Yew continued to work on his toes while Annie-Ting placed her mouth on his fully erected maleness.

After ten minutes of gentle licking and sucking, Annie-Ting and Soot-Yew switched places. Soot-Yew however, was not gentle. She sucked him hard and fast. Sixty seconds after her experienced mouth touched him, his month long build up exploded in her throat. She did not expect such a heavy load. It filled her mouth and throat, causing her to cough. And when she coughed, it spewed not only from her mouth but also through her nose.

Annie-Ting quickly grabbed a towel to clean the client and was disappointed in Soot-Yew for seeming to be unprofessional in what she refers to as – milking the dragon. But Andrew was not complaining, his eyes were closed and he was in a happy place. In fact when he opened his eyes, Soot-Yew's face was already cleaned. He touched it, then gave her a thank you smile.

Annie-Ting realized that they did not lose face, so she spiritedly ushered Andrew to the perfumed bed. Soot-Yew followed and went to the mini-bar to offer him a drink, but he declined.

"No thanks, alcohol makes the dragon sleep."

"Aah!" Soot-Yew and Annie-Ting said simultaneously. Then Soot-Yew picked up a small bottle and asked – "Would you like something to let your dragon rise now?"

Andrew looked at the bottle then replied – "My dragon is just fine, no chemicals needed to make it rise." Then as he pointed at each of them he said with a grin – "Just you – and you". He then held out his hand to Annie-Ting, she took it and went to him. He caressed her full-figured body, then his mouth found her nipples and he sucked on them.

He felt Soot-Yew joined in, her tongue began to pet the dragon. He signaled his plump delight to squat over his face and she did it with exceptional balance for a woman her size. Her fluffy vagina hovered a quart of an inch from his lips and he extended his tongue and licked it.

While he was eating his plump delight, Soot-Yew's mouth was successful in getting Andrew ready again. She opened a condom, saddled the dragon and began to ride him.

His excitement magnified, and then it happened – he tripped. He became Andrew the extremist. That's why he cannot have a quote-unquote 'ordinary woman' in his life. That's why he has to go for therapy. What would people like him do without facilities like Lucky Stem?

Andrew rose up and commanded both women to get on their knees. As they were bent over in front of him, he lubricated his right hand and roughly inserted it in each woman's vagina. A fetish he relishes known as fisting.

He then lubricated their asses and sent his dragon into their caves. Soot-Yew however, surprised him – her narrow cave allowed his dragon to venture to its full length without resistance. Yet, he spent a little more time with Annie-Ting, grinning with every stroke as he enjoyed the bounce of her plump ass.

Just before he ejaculated, he pulled off the condom and had them lay on their backs with their faces under his testicles. Then with a few strokes from his hand, the dragon was milked once again, giving both women an equal amount for their facial.

Andrew felt happy, there isn't anything else that he would rather do to create the sensation that he was feeling. When he checked the time and saw that he had thirty five more minutes to go, he smiled. He then got up from the bed, held their hands and led them to the shower. There, he accepted a steaming oral satisfaction for the duration of his therapy.

Chapter 13

Midnight

DOMONIQUE WAS AWAKE fifteen minutes ago making preparations for the midnight hour. Dressed in her cloak with ceremonial candles lit, she started her chant. Her eyes rolled back and the candle lights flickered. The entity was present with her.

At that very moment a few miles away at New York Presbyterian Hospital, Dr. Sharon Henderson's vitals went haywire. First her temperature went to 104°F, then it dropped to 88°F. Monitors were beeping and Jean-Pierre yelled in a panic – "Nurse!" But they were already running in, and just in time to witness the convulsions.

"What's happening?" Jean-Pierre asked in fright.

"She's having a seizure." One nurse said. Then the other spoke sternly, concerned that he will get in their way. "Sir please step aside or go outside. I already buzzed the doctor, he's on his way."

Jean-Pierre did not want to be forced to leave the room, so he did as he was told.

The doctor walked in just as Jean-Pierre's phone rang.

"Sir you'll have to take that outside, cell phone frequencies can affect our monitors."

Jean-Pierre stepped out and recognized the number to be from his apartment. "Hi mom – dad", he answered not certain which one called but relieved that someone did.

"It's me, how is Sharon? I had a terrible dream." He heard his mother say.

"The doctor is with her now, she had a seizure."

"What! I'll wake your farther, we'll be there soon." She did not give him a chance to object, she just hung up.

Jean-Pierre turned his attention back to Sharon. Through the glass he saw the nurse opened Sharon's gown and the doctor switched on then gelled the defibrillator. Frantic, he rushed to get in but the other nurse stopped him.

"You cannot come in now."

"What's happening to her?"

"She's experiencing cardiac arrest." The nurse explained, before she closed the door.

He watched from the window in horror as Sharon's body jerked from the electric shock. He heard "clear!" then she jerked again then the monitor registered a pulse.

A minute later the doctor came out. He was very direct, definitely not the beat-around-the-bush type.

"Mr. Isaac, I'm Dr. Aaron, we have a situation."

"What is it?" Jean-Pierre asked wide-eyed."

"Two things, one – your fiancée is unconscious and two – the fetal monitor is indicating a problem with the fetus. If we're going to save your baby, then we have to perform a C-section and we have to do it now. The nurses have been told to prep her for the OR. You'll have to suit up if you wish to be present. But I would prefer you wait outside of the OR, just in case you're included in the 4% of the population who are hemophobic. In other words Mr. Isaac, I don't want you to faint. But it's your choice."

"I'll suit up." Jean-Pierre said with confidence, wanting to be as close as possible to Sharon.

"Then follow me" said Dr. Aaron.

Time was critical, in less than ten minutes the doctor and his team were ready to carry out an emergency C-section.

Outside of the OR, Jean-Pierre explained to his parents what the doctor told him. They all prayed for the best, then he went in.

He didn't want to believe that the doctor was right, all he knew was that his legs felt weak. He told himself that he is not part of the 4%, and willed himself to stay conscious. He watched them use a suction machine to remove the blood after the doctor made his incision. Jean-Pierre watched the whole process in amazement. Then finally, the moment came when he heard the doctor asked for a retractor – it was a shiny apparatus used to hold back the tissue. After the head was exposed, the doctor used his hand along with forceps and skillfully took the baby out. The doctor and the observing doctor looked at each other in shock. All six nurses were aghast. One of them quickly used the bulb suction in an attempt to remove the fluid in order for the baby to cry. But she knew it was useless. The doctor frantically took the surgical scissors to cut the black nylon thread that was wrapped so tight around the baby's neck that it sank into the flesh, and made it impossible to cut away without seriously cutting the baby.

Jean-Pierre seemed to have viewed the events in slow motion. The facial expression of the doctors, the nurse's reactions, and the baby's lifeless body, all came together in a rapid reality. Down on his knees he went, tears filled his eyes, his mouth opened but he could not find his voice. And when he did, agony came out. It was the cry of the severely wounded, a cry so deep, that Sharon in her unconscious state heard it and flat-lined.

The doctor scrambled for the defibrillator, gelled it – "clear!"

"Nothing!" the nurse yelled

"We can't lose them both!" One doctor yelled

"Again – clear!" said the one with the defibrillator.

"Nothing"

"She's gone doctor." One nurse said, trusting the long steady beep from the heart monitor. But the doctor looked down at Jean-Pierre who was still on his knees, and overwhelmed with empathy he yelled – "clear!"

Sharon's body jerked for the last time. Dr. Aaron finally accepted – that she was gone.

Jean-Pierre was inconsolable, they allowed him to stay kneeling next to Sharon and his stillborn child as he cried – "No Sharon, no, no."

Everyone were professionals, but they were human first. None of them could have withheld their tears. Jean-Pierre's pain was infectious, even those who were down the hall felt it.

His parents were allowed to go in and grieve with him. They could not say anything. His sorrow was theirs also, so they just embraced.

A nurse who appeared to be in her late forties went to Jeanine and with body language, commanded her attention. Then she spoke softly – "I am from the island of Hispaniola, and I have seen many things." Then she pointed to the baby and said – "Not even the best doctor could have saved them. That is not natural."

Jeanine eyes opened wide when she noticed the black nylon thread that was still around the neck. She suddenly felt dizzy, then she fainted. The nurse held her so she did not hit the floor. Patrick saw her limp body and rushed to her aid.

However, Jean-Pierre – still unable to cope with reality, was holding Sharon's left hand and rubbing the ring with his thumb while saying "I'm sorry Sharon, come back, I'm sorry." He was totally oblivious of his mother's fainting, oblivious of the orderly tapping him on his shoulder offering condolence, but at the same time, telling him that it's time to go, because they have to move the bodies.

Not too far away, the candles went out. Domonique collapsed from exhaustion and crawled to her bed. She mumbled to herself – "It is finished, no more distractions, you're mine now." Then she surrendered to her pillow.

Chapter 14

5:45 – AM

KATHRINE RANG THE bell to the Isaac's home. While she waited she did some knee raises and forward stretches. As she positioned herself to do a side stretch, the door opened.

"Good morning Kathrine."

"Oh, good morning Ana."

"Jeanine will not come with you this morning, there was death in the family. Please call her later." Ana said in her best English then went back inside.

Kathrine left feeling down hearted, because Ana did not tell her who died. But she didn't find any fault in her, after all, it was not her right to divulge Jeanine's business.

After speaking to Kathrine, Ana went to the kitchen to make some lemon and honey tea. She began to sob as she reflected on the early morning event.

It was about 3:30-AM when Ana was awakened by a sound. She was very frighten because she knew she was home alone. Jeanine had called her earlier to inform her, that they will be staying by their son's place to be closer to the hospital. Ana was about to call the police when she heard Patrick's voice say "Get some rest son." Then Jean-Pierre responded "I can't believe they're gone." He sniffled uncontrollably and began to cry. Ana was relieved that it wasn't an intruder, but was sadden for his loss and silently cried for him.

Ana couldn't stop herself, as she sipped her tea the tears ran down her cheeks in a silent race to her lap. However, she did not lend her voice to the melody of the dead. Even though she empathized greatly, for she too have lost loved ones to death.

*****

10:30 – AM

Patrick sat in disbelief as he looked across at Jeanine from their breakfast table. Flabbergasted, he took two gulps of his coffee as he absorbed what she just told him about the baby.

"We have to tell him" he finally said.

"I know, but he doesn't understand these things." Then she added – "I prayed that this day would never come, but he has been found. Now, he must know the truth."

Jeanine stood up and Patrick followed her lead up the stairs. They knocked at Jean-Pierre's door and did not wait for an answer. He was still in bed, just as they knew he would be.

"Come on son it's time to get up. You need to eat something." Said Jeanine as she sat at the edge of his bed.

"I'm not hungry" was the reply in a grief-stricken tone.

Patrick spoke, as if Jeanine tagged him and it was his turn. Very sturdy he said – "Sit up, you need to hear this, sit up now."

Jean-Pierre rarely heard his father speak in a strong tone. When he did, it was always a very serious matter. He sat up with his back leaning against the headboard, and gave his parents his full attention.

Jeanine held his hand and spoke quietly. Her eyes never left his, she wanted him to understand the gravity of the situation.

"What happened to Sharon and your baby was not a normal pregnancy complication."

"I know mom, it's all my fault." Jean-Pierre said and rambled on – "Sharon knew I cheated on her and it placed a lot of stress on her."

"Stop – just stop right there, I know you believe that, but that's not the truth."

Jean-Pierre was about to have another meltdown, so Jeanine got his attention quickly with the cold hard truth. "They were murdered."

Right away his sniffling stopped. He looked into his mother's eyes, then his father's. His father nodded to confirm, then he looked back at his mother and asked – "what do you mean?"

Then she explained "Son you were too distraught to notice the real cause of death. Sharon appeared to have a heart attack, but your baby had a black nylon thread around his neck and was dead before the doctor took him out."

Jean-Pierre commenced giggling like a maniac then said – "I understand that you don't want me to blame myself, but that's the best you can come up with? That doesn't even sound possible."

Patrick was standing with one hand in his pocket. He withdrew it and kept his fist closed as he asked – "Can you see what's in my hand?"

"No"

"What must happen for you to see what's in it?"

"You have to open it, obviously."

"Precisely, and it is the same with the spirit world. You must first open it in order to see all that is possible."

Jeanine interrupted – "Enough is enough, this is going to be painful, but you will not believe until you see for yourself. Let's go to the morgue."

"No, I can't, I can't. I don't want to see her like that." Jean-Pierre said harshly.

Jeanine acknowledged his pain – "OK son, you will not go to the morgue." She said softly while stroking his hand, then added – "But you are taking a trip."

Patrick looked at his wife curiously while Jean-Pierre asked – "Where to?"

"Antigua" then she looked at Patrick and repeated it "Antigua", then added – "I will contact my sister, she will meet you when you land."

Patrick was about to leave then turned and said "We have always told you how special you are, I guess the time has come for you to know exactly how special. I'm sorry tragedy had to strike first." When he turned to leave again, he was halted by Jean-Pierre's words. Because Jean-Pierre did not want to hear how special he is, he felt he was being pressured.

"I'm a grown man, my fiancée just died giving birth to my still born, and you want me to take a trip to the Caribbean, and treat me like I don't have a choice!"

Jeanine chimed in "If you want to know the truth the about what happened, then you don't have a choice. This is the only way son."

Feebly he answered "OK, OK. You win, I'll go." Then his voice changed from whining to purposeful "Since I have to go, the sooner the better, I'm leaving today." Then he sprang out of bed. "Dad I'm going to hit the shower, do me a favor call the store and tell Andrew I'm in mourning, so I'm not taking any calls, just do what he has to do, and I'll see him in a few days. I'll make my travel arrangements when I come down." Then he went to his bathroom and closed his door.

Patrick and Jeanine looked at each other and was certain they thought the same thing. They were stunned by their son's apparent quick recovery. When they left his room, Patrick made his call to the store and Jeanine called her sister.

"Tech World, Andrew speaking."

"Hello Andrew" the voice said gravely – "My son asked me to inform you that he will not be in for the rest of the week. He is mourning the loss of his fiancée and their baby."

Andrew Bridges lips trembled, then he managed to say "No – no – not Dr. Henderson."

"It's a sad time for all of us Andrew, he trust you, hold down the fort, I'll be in touch."

"Of course sir, and my condolence to the family."

"Thank you." Then they hung up.

*****

Noon

When Jean-Pierre stepped out of the house, his mother and father was already seated in the Jaguar. As he place the duffle bag in the trunk, Ana yelled out to him.

"Esperate, Esperate" (wait, wait)

He turned to face her as he closed the trunk.

"Something for you to eat on the plane" she said, then gave him a brown paper bag.

He accepted it "Thank you, it's hot."

"Fresh out of the oven. Have a safe journey." She said, and hugged him.

Jean-Pierre gave her a tight embrace and thanked her again.

Ana's eyes became teary as she watched him drive away. She wasn't sad because he was leaving, she was sad because he was leaving her.

*****

12:45 – PM

At the airport, Jean-Pierre directed his father to the private jet area. When they got there his father stated the obvious. "So you chartered a jet."

"Yes, there were no seats available on the remaining flights today. I didn't want to wait until tomorrow. Besides, it's better this way. It's a straight flight."

Jean-Pierre took the duffle bag from the trunk, then his father wished him a safe trip. His mother's eyes were lachrymose and when she hugged him she started to weep.

"Mom I'll be okay, don't act like it's the first time I'm traveling. What's wrong? You've been quiet for the whole ride."

"It's nothing" she said as she wiped her eyes.

"See you guys when I get back. Oh mom, what does your sister look like?"

"You'll know her when you see her."

After that, he left to be processed and escorted to a Hawker 1000. At the entrance he was greeted by the pilot and co-pilot, along with the stewardess.

"Welcome aboard Mr. Isaac, I'm Senior Captain Watt, this is co-pilot Captain McClean and this is Ms. Young the attendant. It is precisely thirteen hundred hours – we are departing in five minutes and we should have approximately three hours and fifty minutes above the clouds. We will try to make your journey a smooth one. Ms. Young he's all yours."

Jean-Pierre could not help to notice how tall the Senior Captain was. His head almost touch the roof of the cabin. The co-pilot couldn't be missed either. She was a strikingly beautiful dark-skin woman. He gave her a nod, and she nodded back before disappearing into the cockpit. He hoped she understood that was a nod of congratulation, because she is a captain in a male dominated arena.

The stewardess then addressed him – "Mr. Isaac we will be taxiing shortly, please take any seat you like and fasten your seat belt." Ms. Young waited until she heard the 'click!', then she went and closed the cabin door. Afterwards, she sat and buckled herself in.

Jean-Pierre watched through the window and saw the plane began its roll. Five minutes later – airborne.

*****

3:05 – PM

Two hours into his flight, Jean-Pierre rose from his nap.

Ms. Young approached him with a picture perfect smile. "Would you like something to drink Mr. Isaac?"

"Yes, coffee please, a little milk, no sugar. I'm sure what I have here is sweet enough." He said, as he held up the brown paper bag.

"Aah, a little milk, no sugar." She repeated, then volunteered "just how Captain Watt takes it." Then she proceeded to fold out a table and with her million dollar smile, said "I'll be right back."

Jean-Pierre opened the bag and took the aluminum foil wrapped content out. When he opened the foil he smiled. His nose didn't lie, blueberry muffins were before his eyes. Ana packed six of them and Jean-Pierre took a bite before his coffee arrived.

"Here you go sir, if there is anything else I can do for you just let me know."

"Thank you" he said, and continued to eat his muffins.

Jean-Pierre ate all of the muffins, he must have been hungry he thought. Then admitted that they were very tasty.

Ms. Young removed the cup and folded the table back into the panel. Afterwards, Jean-Pierre reclined his seat and closed his eyes to nap for the duration of his flight.

Chapter 15

3:15 – PM

KATHRINE PALOVSKI WAS back in her home after visiting Jeanine. 'Such a misfortune to lose your baby and your fiancée all at once', she thought. She felt sad for her friend for what her son is going through.

Kathrine had a bottle of 1996 Bluegrass Cabernet Sauvignon Magnum, which she was saving for a special occasion. She looked at the rack then spoke to herself – "Well, forget a special occasion, I'm gonna drink with my friend and calm her nerves." She made quick steps to the wine rack. Just as she reached for it, her hand froze. Her momentum interrupted by moans coming from upstairs.

Thinking that Natalya might have fallen reaching for something, she hurried up the stairs. As she got closer to Natalya's room she slowed her pace, recognizing the moans are of a sexual nature. Not fearing that it was George, because he already left for the restaurant, but she proceeded out of sheer curiosity.

Natalya's door was ajarred so Kathrine peeped in. Embarrassed by what she saw, she pulled away. But to confirm what she thought she saw, she peeped again. 'My God' she thought to herself, as she watched Natalya masturbate. 'That dildo must be at least ten inches, how does she fit it all'. Kathrine kept watching Natalya exercise self-gratification. Subconsciously, Kathrine begins to breathe heavily while she touched herself. Just as she realized what she was doing, she composed herself, pulled away from the door then quietly and quickly went back downstairs.

Without any further distractions, Kathrine grabbed the 1996 Bluegrass Cabernet Sauvignon Magnum and went to calm her own nerves with her friend's.

Chapter 16

4:45 – PM

JEAN-PIERRE OBSERVED THE view of their approach to the little island. He did not wait for the stewardess to tell him to fasten his seatbelt. When she heard the 'click!' she smiled and gave him a thumbs-up.

Three minutes later, the Hawker 1000 touched down. It taxied to the terminal for its lone passenger to disembark. 1,785 miles from J. F. K., Jean-Pierre's feet touched the pavement of V. C. Bird International Airport.

Inside the terminal an immigration officer asked him to remove his shades, and he complied. "Wow! Just wanted to see if they're the same as your passport. Welcome home Mr. Isaac, enjoy your stay."

Jean-Pierre looked at him strangely then said – "Thank you, but I don't live here."

The officer returned a strange look of his own along with the passport and said – "I know you don't live here sir, but the place of birth in your document says Antigua." The officer paused for effect then said with a smile – "So – welcome home sir."

The light bulb went on, then he smiled back and thanked the officer. However, Jean-Pierre was a bit concerned that for all the years he has been thought of as the sharpest knife in the draw, was suddenly feeling very dull.

On the way to customs he thought of the many places he have traveled and why didn't his parents encourage him to visit this place, that's obviously considered to be his home.

Customs checked his duffle bag and cleared him.

When Jean-Pierre stepped outside of the terminal, he reflected on his mother's words 'you'll know her when you see her'. He scanned the groups of people awaiting arrivals. There was one woman whom he glimpsed and had to do a double take, after which, his jaw dropped and so did his duffle bag.

The woman was an exact image of his mother. If he did not know better, he would say his mother chartered a faster plane and beat him there.

As she approached him with opened arms he did notice a slight difference. And when they hugged he confirmed it, she was about ten pounds lighter than his mother. But the same oval face, copper tone skin, jet black hair and eyes that were close set yet almost Asian. She continued to hug him as she spoke. And even her voice could be mistaken for his mother's even though his aunt had a trace of French Caribbean flair to hers. "Jean-Pierre I am Jazzel, it is so good to see you after so many years."

Jean-Pierre didn't know what to say, so he said what was appropriate. "I'm sorry I didn't know my mother has an identical twin. I would have gotten to know you sooner."

Jazzel released the embrace and said – "come, my transport is this way."

Minutes later they were inside of a Nissan 4x4 double cab Frontier. Before Jazzel started the vehicle she said. "We're going to my cabin in the hills, it's on the south side of the island at a place call Christian Valley. After we've talked there, we'll go to the house in Blue Waters. It's located on the northern side of the island." Then she started the pickup and they were on their way.

Jean-Pierre rode in silence thinking about Sharon. How could his aunt Jazzel help, - he wondered. At the same time they passed an intersection, Jean-Pierre noticed a sign which read – this way to St. John's, with an arrow pointing right. And this way to Jolly Harbour, with an arrow pointing in the direction they were headed.

Jazzel welcomed the quietness, she had her own conflicting thoughts. Initially, she disagreed with her sister to have Jean-Pierre come to Antigua, but after Jeanine explained what happened, she was left with no other choice but to accept him. She worries how he would handle the truth and if he was ready for the world he was about to be pulled into.

About 30 minutes after they left the airport, Jean-Pierre read a sign that said Christian Valley. His aunt Jazzel turned off the road from which they traveled and onto a dirt road. He observed that they proceeded pass a poultry farm, then a variety of tropical fruit trees. Then onto another dirt road which took them to a dense wooded area.

"Nous sommes ici." (We are here), Jazzel said.

Jean-Pierre stepped out of the pickup and looked around. "Where is the cabin?"

"Right this way" she said smiling. And as she took the lead on the narrow path, Jean-Pierre grabbed his duffle bag and followed her for two minutes to a clearing in the woods. There he saw the cabin. It was surrounded by dwarf fruit trees of all kinds in different sized containers. He didn't know the names of them all, but in his mind he named what he recognized.

Inside they sat at a round table which had only 3 chairs. She offered tea and he declined. Two minutes later she brought the cup and set it in front of him. "This will help you to be calm, you are anxious, and Jean-Pierre you can take your shades off now, you are inside."

"What kind of tea is this?"

"Marijuana"

"Isn't that illegal?"

"Under who's law? Hmm, the plant was around before man said it is illegal. And the same man that rendered it a crime, knows of its medicinal power and uses it, leaving the foolish to abide by the law and get sick then die. Now drink your tea, and when you are finished I need you to listen to what I have to tell you."

It was 5:50 PM, Jean-Pierre felt powerless. He obeyed his mother and took this trip, then against his desire he drank marijuana tea. He hoped it was all worth it he thought, as he put the empty cup down.

Jazzel sat across the table from Jean-Pierre, she looked into his eyes then she began.

"It is so wonderful to look into those eyes again. Your heterochromia is not a birth defect, it is a gift. And speaking of defects, it leads me to the beginning of the story. My sister and I were born with a defect that caused the development of endometriosis. We did not know this prior to her getting married. When she became aware of her condition and informed me, I had the test done and discovered that I too was infertile. Patrick was a good man, he accepted my sister as she was. But I – I could not accept myself. I had dreams of becoming a mother and I refused to let some doctor tell me that I could not. I was young and beautiful, and I invited many men to my bed in hope of a fluke. When all failed I resorted to greater powers. I went back to my homeland of Guadeloupe. There, I sort the intervention of a woman known to me as Madam Salis. For one week she fed me only with nuts, berries and raw leafy vegetables. Some were bitter, I did not know their names at that time. On the first day of the new week she gave me a bitter substance to drink and for the entire day she did not feed me, she only lit incense and chanted. Then one hour before midnight she filled a metal bath with warm water and different leaves then gave me what she called a bush bath. Then she had me lay down naked on a round table the height of a coffee table. She said she needed to bind my hands and feet because moving would interrupt the process, so I let her. My hands were bound above my head and my feet were bound spread apart. Then she lit candles on the floor in a circle around us. She danced and from a nearby sack removed a rooster. It was perfectly timed, because the midnight hour came just as she removed an amulet which I later learned it to be the Triangle of Solomon and placed it on the table next to me. Right after, with her bare hands she removed the head of the rooster. The warm blood was sprinkled onto me, then onto the amulet. She called three names that I should not repeat, then she tilted her head back, held the twitching rooster above her face and drank its blood. Within ten seconds she removed her clothes. I assure you it was a woman who stood before me with a vagina like mine and breast like mine, but her eyes were not hers anymore. When she mounted me it was a man I felt inside of me, a big man hurting me. It felt like forever but her assistant said it was more like three minutes. When it was over, Madam Salis couldn't move. Her assistant carried her to her room and later returned to clean me up. It took her two days to recover. When she did, she asked me to stay until the baby was born. I told her that I didn't even know if it worked and my friends will worry if I'm gone for so long. I saw that she felt offended about me saying not certain if it worked. Anyway, she allowed me to go and advised me to let her know what my physician says in thirty days.

Well I was with child, and as promised I notified her. But when I asked how much I had to pay, she said it would not be much and I shouldn't worry about it now. As time passed I forgot about the payment and was only thinking of motherhood. But one week before my baby was born I got a message from the assistant that Madam Salis will be sending her to collect the payment. When I told her that it was not necessary to travel, that I will send the money, she simply said Madam Salis will be sending her to collect the payment when the child is born. I thanked her from the bottom of my heart because she risked her life to tell me that the payment was my child. I cried because I didn't know what to do, but I had to protect my baby."

Jazzel paused to compose herself. The pain she buried so long ago has resurfaced. She continues – "When he was born I looked into his beautiful eyes, one blue the other gray and I held him just for a moment before giving him to the only other person beside myself that I trust to keep him safe, my beloved twin. I told Jeanine that she had to leave right away. You were too young to fly so her and her husband took you by boat to the Virgin Islands. Then from there when you were stronger, a flight to New York. It was then I took on the task of becoming wise in the craft, so I could keep them from you. But they found you son, so now you have to learn to use your gifts."

Jean-Pierre had tears in his eyes. He felt the tremendous love Jazzel had for him. To go through so much to have him, then to give him up to save him. "Mom" he said – "It doesn't feel weird calling you that. I guess looking alike helps." Then he asked – "what do they want me for?"

"They don't want you now son, you have your own mind. They would not be able to control you as if they had you from birth. Now, they want your first born."

"If they wanted my first born then why did they kill him?"

"Because they must already have a host who is willing to give up the child."

With that said, Jazzel quickly got up and filled a silver bowl with water. She returned and placed it on the table's center then commanded – "Give me your finger."

He wasn't sure which finger she wanted, so he gave her his hand. After she took it, he felt a prick on his index finger, but from what – he did not know.

She squeezed it, causing a drop of his blood to mix in the water. Then she said words that were unfamiliar to him. Clearly they were not words from the eight languages that he speaks. Then she said – "Look into the vessel and tell me what you see."

"This is amazing, how did you...never mind. I see women whom I've been intimate with."

"What else do you see?"

"They're walking from one side of the bowl to the next then vanish."

"The image that remains is of the one who caused your grief, and is the same one chosen to carry your first born."

Jean-Pierre watched as if watching a television screen, the images crossed and disappeared. When Domonique's face came into view, it remained. Jean-Pierre was so livid, he screamed into the silver vessel at the face that once enticed him.

"I see you've found her" Jazzel said, then stood up to take a closer look. She was taken aback and gasped.

Jean-Pierre noticed the recognition and asked "Do you know Domonique?"

"She is the daughter of madam Salis. She must not be allowed to have your seed."

"It might be too late" he said regretfully, adding "We copulated without any caution."

"Don't be downhearted son, you were beguiled and it's not too late."

Jean-Pierre tried to wrap his head around it all, but could not.

"I thought magic and witchcraft were fairy tales, and people who actually believed in them were delusional."

Jazzel tried to console him and also push him in the direction she needed him to go.

"Jean-Pierre, I'm sorry for your loss. It was a cruel way for you to find out the hidden reality of this world. But the power is in your hand to chart your destiny or to pretend you don't know what you do know now and have it charted for you."

"But what can I do? I don't have a clue about this black magic stuff." He said with naivety.

Jazzel laughed at how he said that, then explained. "Well your first lesson is – there is no 'black' or 'white' magic, it's just magic. It is the action of the erudite which is either good or bad.

Black and white, those are just propaganda for you to associate black with evil and white with good. A subliminal way to get people of a darker skin to believe that they are less than their lighter counterparts. Furthermore, this is a secret art. It's not to be toyed with and make mock like those who entertain and call themselves magicians."

Jean-Pierre hung on to every word proceeded from Jazzel's mouth. He acknowledged and accepted his fate as flashes of Sharon's smiling face crossed his mind, to be replaced by flashes of her comatose state and final tears. Those images pushed him to a dangerous place, they magnified a loath for Domonique which can only be quelled by the exact measure she meted out to Sharon. He looked up at Jazzel with determined eyes and eagerness in his voice – "What's the next lesson?"

A hopeful Jazzel answered with a smile – "Now we go to Blue Waters."

Chapter 17

7:10 –PM

THE SUNSET WAS beautiful, but Jean-Pierre did not see its magnificence. He was preoccupied with wanting to know more about his special gift. Being he was – according to his mother's account – spiritually conceived.

They were standing on the balcony of Jazzel's home in Blue Waters, north of the island, looking over Soldier Bay. She pointed north – "Tonight we go there."

Jean-Pierre looked in the direction and saw nothing but the ocean, so he inquired – "what's there?"

"Barbuda – now get some rest, I will wake you when it's time."

"I'm not tired. Tell me more, like why do you live alone in such a big house and still have a cabin in the hills."

Jazzel chuckled before answering – "The path that I've chosen is a lonely path. The discipline which comes with the knowledge I possess makes it difficult to find a partner that is compatible. As for this house, it was purchased after you picked the winning numbers for my sister. I invested wisely, so what she sent me was enough to sustain me even to this day. As for the cabin, it happens to be on my farm. I like to grow my own food especially since I'm a vegetarian. But the cabin serves another purpose – seclusion." As she said 'seclusion' she pointed to another beach front property about 200ft away and said "no neighbors to see my business."

Jean-Pierre and his mother spoke for hours on a variety of issues, then she looked to the stars and said – "It's time".

She led the way down to the beach. Jean-Pierre looked around perplexed then asked – "So – where's the boat?"

"There are better ways to travel" Jazzel assured as she stooped down to trace a circle in the sand. It was about 3 feet in diameter, and within it she drew symbols which appeared to be a combination of Arabic and Egyptian hieroglyphics. Then she stood up and held his hand. Looking into his eyes she said – "Step in with me, do not be afraid. This is how we travel." Together, facing the ocean they stepped into the circle. Jean-Pierre heard his mother say a few words, then felt a strong breeze which lifted some sand. He closed his eyes to avoid any particles, when the wind subsided he opened them and the ocean was to their backs.

"Wow! This is amazing. How did we ... I mean you do that?"

"I will not explain it to you now because you will not understand. You have to be awakened first, for everything to become clear to you."

She signaled him to follow and they walked for less than quart of a mile, then entered a cave.

Jean-Pierre did not say he was afraid but his own words exposed him. "It was dark enough out there, now I can't see a thing in here. Are you going to light something?"

"Shh! Patience." She commanded.

They stood quietly in the dark. Then suddenly, a blue sphere of light appeared in the distance and in the blink of an eye it was in front of them.

Jean-Pierre did not know if he imagined what he saw, but there seemed to be a little man inside the light. Then a whispering voice said – "come".

They followed the floating sphere which kept a distance of twenty feet ahead of them. As they walked in silence, Jean-Pierre seemed to be spooked by the disturbed bats when they flew past. After about an hour, they came upon a pool and Jazzel said to him – "I cannot come any further, this is your journey. Do not be afraid."

Then the voice from the sphere spoke again, but this time not in a whisper – "The knowledge that you are about to receive should be guarded and not abused. I sense your desire for vengeance, but be forewarned, acts of kindness will enhance you and acts of wickedness will consume you. Use wisdom to solve a problem, justice does not have to be life for life. Now follow me and do not fear death, for you are dead already."

The sphere went into the water and illuminated it. Jean-Pierre followed until he was neck deep. Then the sphere plunged deeper, and Jean-Pierre held his breath then dove to follow. He believed he would end up in some kind of underwater cavern to get air, but all he saw was the light in front of him and the voice saying – "we're almost there". With confidence he pressed on, but at the same time his heart raced with anxiety and his lungs were desperate for air. He glanced towards the surface and knew he could not make it if he turned back. So he looked to the light, involuntarily inhaled and blacked out.

The little man whom Jean-Pierre thought he imagined, sat crossed legged in the sphere looking at the sinking corpse.

The sphere then went to the body and touched its head. A light went through Jean-Pierre and he opened his eyes. They glowed while he received instructions without words. Thereafter an orb was formed around him, then he too sat with his legs crossed.

The two spheres surfaced and glided to Jazzel. Jean-Pierre's vanished and he landed on his feet. She was pleased to see the glow in his eyes, an enlightenment which surpassed many, including her own.

She bowed to the blue sphere and turned to leave, but was halted by the voice.

"Young one, do not get overzealous with your gift and forget the wise counsel of your mother. Finally – you must be one hundred percent faithful when carrying out a task, because one percent of doubt will prevent the manifestation of your desire." After that was said, the blue light was gone.

Jean-Pierre and Jazzel exited the cave. When they arrived at the beach, Jean-Pierre wanted to open the portal, but his mother advised against it. "When we have the time son, but now is not the time. The wrong formula can take us to a completely different place, and even worse, can invite an evil entity that can destroy us."

Jean-Pierre was eager to apply the knowledge he was given, and insisted – "But I know what I'm doing, I can see everything clearly in my head."

"Okay then, I'll open my own door, see you on the other side."

Jazzel stooped and made her marking in the sand, stepped into her circle, spoke and disappeared.

Jean-Pierre did the same and he also vanished from the beach of Barbuda.

Just as Jazzel was about to walk from the beach to her house, she heard splashing in the water behind her. She looked back to see Jean-Pierre about 15 feet from shore. She wanted to laugh, but did not, this was a serious matter. His calculations were a little off. But that in itself can be dangerous.

When he reached the shore she made sure to remind him of the warning – "Remember what the light said about being overzealous, you could have ended up in the middle of the ocean."

"I'm sorry" he said, not wanting her to be upset. Then thought to himself – 'but I was close' – and smiled.

Inside the house Jazzel advised her son to leave Domonique for a few weeks and not to let on that he has been awakened.

Then she reminded him that he has to return the same way in which he came, in order for his passport to reflect his departure.

He was disappointed in hearing both, but he understood. The private jet company he used has a 24 hours, 7 days a week service. So he was not surprised that at 1:00 AM someone answered the phone to assist him with a flight.

5:45 AM

Jean-Pierre hugged his mom and kissed her forehead. "Thank you, I exist because of you. Je t'aime (I love you)"

"Et je t'aime trop (I love you too)"

After their exchange in French, he checked in and boarded the Hawker 1000, meeting the same crew. He smiled and took a seat. At exactly 0600 hours the plane taxied down the runway and at 130 mph it lifted off. Jean-Pierre looked out of the window until he could no longer see the little island of 108 square miles.

Chapter 18

7:00 AM

JEANINE RETURNED FROM her morning walk to find Patrick sipping on tea in the living room.

"Oh, you're up, you should have joined me for the walk."

"Your sister called."

"Jeanine's heart skipped a beat and she went closer to him then asked – "Is everything alright?"

"Fantastic, I have to go to the airport for our son, his flight lands in 3 hours."

"I don't understand, he was only gone for a day."

"Well she said that they went to Barbuda and he saw the light."

Jeanine did not respond. She knew what was meant by 'he saw the light', Patrick however, did not. But he was not a stranger to the supernatural.

When Patrick was a small boy, he fell ill with a fever that would not break. His parents although Christians like many people on the island, sort the help of an obeah-man. The obeah-man or woman was the secret spiritual advisor to many who claimed they were Christians. The obeah-man got rid of the fever and explained it was their neighbor who caused it, because she envied the child's excellence in school over her child. When they were asked what should be done, Patrick's father in anger requested for the sickness to be sent to the woman's child. But his mother intervened and said the child was innocent just like theirs, so send the sickness back to the sender. It was done, then two days later their neighbor fell ill and did not recover.

Jeanine looked across towards the kitchen. The fresh smell of muffins caught her nose. Patrick saw that look of scent recognition on her face.

"That's right, blueberry muffins. I told Ana that Jean-Pierre was coming back today. I did not tell her to make the muffins. I guess she knows he likes them" he said smiling.

"And I know he's not the only one that likes them," she responded, and pinched him tummy, then said "you better start walking with me in the mornings." She then went upstairs to prepare to accompany him to the airport.

*****

10:10 AM

Jean-Pierre walked from the private jet area to where his parents were parked. When he reached them, he dropped his duffle bag and embraced them both at the same time. "I love you mom and dad. I had the most incredible experience, but I'll tell you about it another time. Right now I want to say, I am what I am, because of her. But I am who I am because of you. Now let's go, because we have to get to the crematorium."

"The crematorium?" Jeanine and Patrick asked together.

"Yes, I called them from the plane, they are going to the morgue to retrieve the body."

"Son isn't that too sudden?" Jeanine asked.

"No mom, her death was too sudden." - Jean-Pierre answered, and the thought of Sharon's dead body almost brought him to tears.

Inside the car, he gave his father the direction – "It's the crematorium in midtown on 152nd E 28th Street." Then Jean-Pierre sniffed, and said "Wait, am I smelling muffins?"

Patrick laughed as Jeanine answered and passed the bag, "here you go son, Ana made them, but you're short of one." Then she tilted her head towards Patrick, indicating that he's the culprit.

"Speaking of Ana, didn't you want her there?" Jeanine asked.

"Not really mom, she has been through a lot, and I didn't want my grief to open her old wounds."

Jeanine nodded her head then said, "That's very considerate son, I didn't think of that."

They then drove part of the way with him explaining about Domonique and the other part in silence.

*****

11:15 AM

Inside of the crematory's chapel was decorated in purple and gold. The director greeted Patrick and his family when they walked in – "Good day, I'm director Haslemere, how may I be of service?"

"I'm Jean-Pierre Isaac, I spoke with you this morning."

"Ah Mr. Isaac, right this way please."

They were lead down a corridor with a door with a name plate which read 'Johnathan Haslemere DIRECTOR.' There were a few chairs outside of the office.

"I only need Mr. Isaac's signature on some documents, so please wait here." And he gestured to Patrick and Jeanine to the chairs.

The color scheme in the office was the same purple and gold. Jean-Pierre stopped observing as the director began to speak.

"This one is the application for a cremation permit, this one – the authorizing agent, which you are and this is the bill, all fees included, which you have taken care of when you gave me your card number this morning."

Jean-Pierre signed everything and was given a receipt.

"Thank you Mr. Isaac. We will have a brief ceremony as you've requested, also the bodies have been placed as you've requested. After the ceremony the actual cremation will take place later today upon receipt of the permit. Then, at a time of your convenience you can collect the ashes. And if you haven't done so already, we have a wonder selection of urns to choose from."

Jean-Pierre thanked him, then they joined his parents in the corridor. On their way to the chapel, Jean-Pierre informed the director that the priest would not be needed, because his fiancée was not a Catholic. They simply preferred to have some time alone.

In the chapel the director excused the priest and honored the bereaved family's wish.

As they held hands in silence Jean-Pierre released his parent's hands and placed his hands on the chestnut colored casket. His lips trembled and he folded them in to hold back his voice, but he could not hold back the tears from streaming down his cheeks.

Patrick hugged his wife as he buried her face in his chest to weep. Then he noticed Jean-Pierre opening the casket. "No son" he whispered, knowing that seeing the body would be the catalyst to another melt-down.

Jean-Pierre looked at Sharon in the pose he request. Her hands clutching their baby to her bosom as if they were both sleeping. But he looked back at her hand, because something didn't seem right. "The ring" he said to himself, and seemed to become sober from his hysteria.

Jean-Pierre stormed to the director and was demanding to know what happened to the engagement ring. But Jonathan Haslemere understood his client's distress and answered softly.

"Mr. Isaac I assure you that nothing has been removed from your loved ones once they were in our care. We have an impeccable customer service record, in addition, jewelries are amongst the list of items that cannot be cremated. It would have been removed and presented to you. Perhaps you should investigate the facility we collected the bodies from."

"Thank you Mr. Haslemere, I will."

Patrick and Jeanine had followed Jean-Pierre, therefore heard the dialogue and without anything else to say, they left the crematorium.

In the car Jean-Pierre asked his father to take him to his apartment and leave him there and he would meet them at the house later.

*****

Noon

When Jean-Pierre opened the door to his apartment, he stood at its entrance with his duffle bag in hand and felt the stark reality of stepping into what he sees as an empty home – a home without Sharon. He went to their bedroom to put away his bag and saw the sweatshirt she wore a few nights ago hanging on a hook outside of her closet. He walked slowly to hit and held it. He removed it from it from its place then sat at the edge of the bed and caressed it as one would caress a pet. He placed it to his face to feel the fabric against his cheeks. Then he inhaled deeply, traces of Shalimar perfume mixed with her scent instigated memories of precious moments. He folded it neatly placed his next to his pillow, not wanting so soil it with his tears.

Jean-Pierre's voice was sorrowful, he spoke as if Sharon was next to him. "I am sorry for the roll I played in what happened to you." Then his voice changed to rage. Speaking slow and calculated, he said "But the one who's responsible for taking you and our son from this world, will – not – escape – her – KARMA!"

Jean-Pierre took his riding jacket and helmet, then he exited his apartment. His first mission – retrieve the ring.

*****

12:30 PM

New York Presbyterian Hospital had its usual air of busyness. Jean-Pierre was talking to the admin staff who previously gave him the visitor's pass, Ms. S. Cox.

"So you said the orderly is on duty now?"

"Yes, I can call him to this location and you can speak with him privately in that room over there." She said, pointing to room G13.

Jean-Pierre thanked her and turned to go to the room. Then he heard "tragedy can make the strongest of us lose focus and become discombobulated. You don't remember me do you?" He looked at her features deeper, searching his memory, because her tone suggested he met her before she gave him the visitor's pass. 'What does the 'S' stand for, he repeated in his mind, then blurted out "Soni, its Soni right?"

She smiled and said "yes, I sat behind in science class." She saw that he was happy for the recollection, but she knew his thoughts were on business and waved him along as she made the call.

The two hundred and seventy pounds orderly with dirty blond hair entered room G13. His round eyes met Jean-Pierre's shaded eyes.

"How may I help you?" – He asked.

"It's a private matter, close the door please."

The orderly did as he was asked, then took the hand that extended to him.

"I'm Jean-Pierre Isaac."

"Eric Schwartz." The orderly said and tried to release his hand, but Jean-Pierre held it as he stated his purpose. "I'm here to ask you about a ring." Through his hand, Jean-Pierre felt the man's increased heart rate before he suddenly pulled away.

"I don't know what you're talking about, what ring?" he asked. Only to fool himself when he feigned ignorance, because his aura already revealed the truth to Jean-Pierre.

"Eric do you think it's by chance I am hear talking to you? The last thing you want to do is to piss of someone who is already pissed off at someone else. Because you Mr. Schwartz will then receive the full force of that person's wrath. Am I clear?"

Eric raised both hands chest level with palms facing Jean-Pierre and started to plea. "Wait – wait, let me explain."

Jean-Pierre contained his anger, he did not want an explanation, only the ring, but he gave him his ear. "Go on."

Eric was so afraid that he forgot to be mindful of words that may be insensitive. "I told my friend Frankie that I saw this diamond on a dead black chick that's gotta worth at least twenty grand. He told me that his uncle controls a pawn shop in Brooklyn so fencing it wouldn't be a problem. But when I came into work this morning the memo said that the body is being moved to a crematorium. I took that as a sign that it's okay to take it. After all, you can't burn diamonds, and besides, Frankie says the dead don't need no bling."

Jean-Pierre's patience was running thin and maybe Eric must have sensed that, because his hand was swift in going into his pocket to retrieve the ring.

Jean-Pierre held the ring and examined it, then he gave Eric a warning.

"You seem to have a problem thinking for yourself. You listen to Frankie a lot but Frankie is not your friend, he's a loafer who wants you to lose your job to join him in doing nothing and being nothing. Change your friend or you future will be very dim. You and Frankie could be spending a lot of time together in a facility not of your choosing."

After his words of caution, Jean-Pierre left the room noting that Mr. Schwartz was not apologetic, neither did he express gratitude for him not calling the police in an obvious case of larceny. He concluded that the lack of wisdom will cause Schwartz to meet his fate.

Chapter 19

1:30 – PM

JOHNNY SANTIAGO WAS early for his after school job. "Hey Johnny you had a half day today?" Marsh asked him.

"Sort of." he answered, and proceeded to put away his bag.

Andrew Bridges saw the look that went with the tone, a look he knew all too well. "Johnny, I'd like to see you in the office. Angeline, take over the register please."

Andrew saw in the chair behind the glass desk and looked at the person he was asked to help mentor. He did not beat around the bush. "So what happened in school today?"

"What do you mean?"

"I know that look of defeat Johnny, it's just us, so tell me."

"Those guys that I was with when I first came in here, they teamed up with some bullies in school and they wanted me to join them after school to bully a freshman. I didn't want to do so I left early."

Andrew nodded in agreement of Johnny's action then verbalized it. "You did the right thing. You never know when a victim will say enough is enough, and everyone involved will receive a payback in the worst possible way. And usually when shit hits the fan, cowards run and leave the people they pulled into to smell it by themselves. It was brave of you to take a stand for what you believe in."

Andrew looked into his eyes and confessed to him. "I used to get bullied. I can tell you many stories, but that will take too long so I'll just tell you this one. When I was in the sixth grade there was a little Indian kid by the name of Bulan, I thought he was my friend. One day he offered me some chocolate and said it was a new candy bar. He took it from the outer wrapper and broke it in half, giving me six of the squares and keeping six for himself. He watched me consumed mine and said he was saving his for later. The little chocolate squares had the name Ex-lax on them. I never heard of it before. I told him it didn't taste bad. Twenty minutes after the class started, my hand was raised to be excused for the bathroom. All those who were involved laughed. By the time I came back, two minutes later, my hand was raised again. When laughter broke out, the teacher denied me because he thought I was being a class clown. When I couldn't hold it any longer I got up without permission and ran for the door. But it was too late, by the time my hand touched the knob to exit the class, I had no control, shit came out my ass. The girls were repulsed and guys all laughed. It took the rest of the week to gather the nerves to go back to school. Bulan told me he was sorry. He said that they told him, if he helped them to prank me, they would stop bullying him. So Johnny, it is good of you to stand up for what you believe in, but beware, that now they may want to bully you."

"Thank you for sharing that with me, I hear the hurt in your voice as you recount the event. I will be careful. Thank you."

Then they left the office and went about their duties.

Chapter 20

4:00 – PM

JEAN-PIERRE SPED THROUGH the Queens Midtown Tunnel after leaving the crematorium. Sharon's ashes were in a box strapped to the seat under a cargo net. Taking the 495 straight to exit 17W, then unto Laurel Hill Blvd. Then a series of left and right turns to end up at Green Point Avenue, at First Calvary Cemetery. A trip that should have taken thirty minutes took the skilled rider fifteen.

Jean-Pierre unfastened the box of ashes and walked about sixty yards to a grave with a tombstone which read James and Ligaya Henderson – they were Sharon's parents. They died three years ago in a car accident on the Clearview Expressway.

Teenagers at times played games that leads to fatality. Such was the case with Mr. and Mrs. Henderson. A group of teenagers played a game of Target from the pedestrian overpass. Some had eggs and some had rocks. They agreed on a car and then they all took aim. The Henderson's were startled by the rain of rocks and eggs that shattered and smeared the windshield. The assault caused a loss of control and the vehicle somersaulted several times before it landing on its roof, killing both occupants.

Jean-Pierre opened the box and said "She was the only part left from the both of you, I'm sorry I couldn't save her." Then he sprinkled Sharon's and the baby's ashes on her parents grave.

Jean-Pierre did not shed any more tears. His eyes seemed to glow from rage. He left the empty box by the tombstone and took a frustrated walk back to his bike, because all he could think about was how to deal with Domonique.

His mother advised him to let a few weeks pass before taking action. But he doesn't feel he could hold off that long.

The Kawasaki started and Jean-Pierre left the cemetery and headed towards University Gardens.

*****

6:00 – PM

Domonique sat at a table for two in a French restaurant on Ludlow Street, on the lower East side of Manhattan. She stared on her hors d'oeuvres as she waited for the l'agneau (lamb) as the main course. She did not expected her invited guest to show, because he did return her call after her message of invitation. He must still be in mourning, she thought as she took another bite of Quiche Lorraine. After she swallowed before taking another bite, she said audibly enough for her ears alone "Pas de probleme mon amour, je vais attendre jusqu'a ce que vous récupérer de votre désespoir, puis tu es á moi." (No problem my love, I'll wait until you recuperate from your despair, then you are mine.)

At the same time in University Gardens, Jean-Pierre gave his parents an account of what happened when he went to the hospital. Then he told them about the message from Domonique. "I could not respond to her message. I don't think that I could pretend that I don't know what she did. So it's best that I keep my distance until I am ready to face her in the realm that she lives in."

Jean-Pierre went to pour some water from a glass bottle he imported from Tasmania. Then Jeanine asked, "So what will you do to Domonique?"

"I'm still working that out in my head. I'm trying to see how to remove her from the land of the living."

Jeanine gasped, Patrick just sat and listened then he heard his wife say "You have to remember son in life when you do good, good comes back to you, and it goes the same way with evil deeds."

Jean-Pierre raised his voice "Really mom, I'm tired of that rhetoric! Tell me what evil Sharon did to deserve what happened to her?"

Patrick jumped in, his voice calm but stern, "I know you're upset, but you are talking to your mother, watch your tone."

"Jé suis dé solée mama (I'm sorry mom) I guess this is what Sharon would call displaced aggression."

"I understand son, apology accepted." Jeanine said.

"I feel tired, I think I'll take a nap before going for Ana."

"It's okay son, she took a cab to go. She will take one to come, get your rest." Patrick said.

"I can't sleep for too long dad, so I don't mind. Anyway, I have my thoughts on sinking my teeth in some burritos.

"You're going to Taco Bell?" His mother asked.

"Oui (yes)"

"Then you can bring back a beef taco for me." She said

Patrick was not about to be left out. "All this talk about Taco Bell, just rang my 'it's time to eat bell'. Come on honey lets go, my stomach don't want to wait till he comes back."

"See you later son" Jeanine said and left with Patrick.

Jean-Pierre did not bother going to his room, instead he fell asleep right there on the couch.

On the way to Taco Bell Jeanine expressed her concern to her husband. "I have to call my sister, she's the only one who can stop him."

"Stop him from doing what?" Patrick asked, disturbed by his wife's statement.

"Come on Pato, weren't you paying attention? Didn't you see the look in his eyes when he said he wants to remove Domonique from the land of the living?"

"Well if that's how he feels don't you think he is well within his right to feel that way?"

"Yes, but I don't want our son to commit murder."

"The choice is his Jeanine, stay off the spiritual battle field. We lead him to this point, now trust that his morals are intact and back off."

"But this has nothing to do with morals Pato, this is about justice and revenge."

"There you go, you said it, justice. So let it go Jeanine, let it go."

She was quite for the duration of the drive to Taco Bell, but in her private thoughts Jeanine already decided that she would contact her sister.

*****

7:15 – PM

Jean-Pierre didn't know exactly how, but he sensed a change in the atmosphere and decided not to use the motorcycle. When he stepped out of the house and saw precipitation, he smiled as he twirled the Porsche's key ring around his finger. It was a smile of acknowledgement that he was in tune with the four elements.

The engine revved, and the black Porsche 911 cruised from University Gardens before acceleration on the parkway in the direction of H.L.I.

Twenty five minutes later Jean-Pierre waited outside of Hillcrest Learning Institute. He closed his eyes as he listened to the Lenny Kravitz album Sharon gave to him. 'I Belong To You' was playing, it was her favorite track. The CD was set to repeat and he was in another place and time until the tap on the glass broke his daydream.

Ana smiled and waved, then Jean-Pierre touched the unlock switch to let her in. As soon as she sat down, she said "thank you for coming. Guess who got a 100% on her English oral exam."

"Congrats. I was going to Taco Bell, but if you want to go somewhere to celebrate..."

Ana didn't let him finish his thought – "No its ok, I think I'll eat a taco."

Jean-Pierre was pleased, he was really in the mood for a burrito. He switched the track to 'Fly Away' then they were off to Taco Bell.

Chapter 21

Midnight

UNIVERSITY GARDENS WAS quiet, and even though the night was still and the windows closed, Jean-Pierre was awakened by a sudden gust of wind. For a second he thought his eyes deceived him. There was a six feet in diameter hole on a wall in his bedroom. It looked like a mirror except it wasn't his room in its reflection. Jazzel was also in there with an out-stretched hand, and he heard her say to him – "you're not dreaming, come son, quickly."

Jean-Pierre became surprisingly alert and sprang from his bed then reached for his mother. He felt the warmth of her hand and knew he was with her. He looked back and caught a glimpse of his room before the portal closed.

Upon observing his new environment, Jean-Pierre realized it wasn't new at all. He was standing in Domonique's bedroom. He did not ask how, and he did not think it was impossible. Jean-Pierre was in a comfortable place of acceptance – acceptance of the bizarre and wonderful world of sorcery.

He watched Domonique lay motionless. "Is she dying?" he asked Jazzel with an anxious voice.

"No, and her blood will not be on my hands or yours. Understand this son, whatever curses follows her will transfer and follow whoever cancels her life."

"Then why am I here?" he asked annoyed.

"To observe, you have the power son but not the emotional discipline." Jazzel walked over to Domonique then turned her attention back to Jean-Pierre – "This is a spell of paralysis, she can see and feel everything, but she cannot move. It will feel like a nightmare she's experiencing, yet cannot wake from it. But knows without a shadow of a doubt it is real."

Turning her focus back to Domonique, Jazzel raised Domonique's night gown to expose her nakedness. She then placed one hand between the navel and pelvis, and the other stretched towards the sky. Then she spoke –
"Just as the days of old
When the Nile River ran red
Just as the fullest moon
Shined like millions have bled
Just as it went in, it will come out in this bed"
Domonique started to convulse, and when the shaking stopped, blood flowed from her vagina. Jazzel then removed a small vile from a pouch and poured its content in Domonique's mouth then said – "I bind you witch without words to tell, I bind you witch from ever casting spells."

Steam came from Domonique's mouth along with a sizzling sound. Curious, Jean-Pierre asked his mother what was in the vile, and he cringed when she replied – "acid".

Jazzel then drew a circle around Domonique, after the symbols and words, Domonique disappeared, but not before Jean-Pierre saw the tears in her pretty green eyes.

Jean-Pierre looked at his mother thankfully and said – "So you sent her back to Madam Salis."

"Yes, and the paralysis is temporary, but she will never speak again. Without her tongue, she is powerless."

Jazzel hugged him and reminded him – "don't forget son, each month when the moon is at its fullest, you must dip in our water seven times before the Sun rises."

"I remembered, and I know how to get back to my room – see you next month mom."

*****

6:10 – AM

George Palovski laid dreamily when he felt the warm body entered the bed and caressed his scrotum. He smiled as he thought how wonderful it was for his wife to come back to bed for an early morning romp instead of her usual exercise with Jeanine. Wet lips touched the tip of his standing shaft and slowly blanketed it to its base. Up and down she moved her head giving him that feeling that he loves. The heat of her throat, lips and tongue, and not too much teeth. "Mmm" he moaned, followed by "Jeanine might be mad that you skipped out on her, but I'm not."

George held her head to caress it and felt something strange. Kathrine's hair was to her nape, instead of her shoulders. He opened his eyes to ask her when she got a trim and his heart almost jumped out of his chest.

"Oh shit Natalya!"

Her eyes did not turn from his, and she engaged him with greater intensity. The pleasure she gave him numbed his brain, and caused him to stutter.

"You – you – you ...have t – t – to ... st... st... stop."

But his stuttering words of protest were meaningless, because his erection contradicted them along with his failure to pull himself away or push her away. Instead, George continued to caress her head, and moaned "Mmm".

It was Natalya who decided to stop. She rose up and straddled him, but did not put him inside of her.

"Are you ready for me?" She teased.

And George shook his head like a drooling puppy.

"Touch my pussy." She commanded. And he did. The slippery moisture on his fingers screamed 'ready for sex', but Natalya did not give it. Instead, she teased him some more.

"Show me that you're the king of your castle. Let me see how talented you are in convincing your wife to submit to your desire of a ménage á trois. Do that, and it will be more than your fingers getting wet inside of me."

Natalya then slowly dismounted and with a supermodel's gait, made her exit from his room, with two thoughts in mind. 'Men are so predictable, and how George will open the door to her finally spooning Kathrine'.

One hour later, Kathrine returned from her exercise to meet George coming out of the shower. "What are you doing up so early?" she asked.

"It wasn't by choice, I had a weird dream."

"About what?"

He paused before answering "We had a ménage á trois, and guess what, you liked it."

"Really – that's why it was a dream." She replied, killing the seed he planted.

He approached her and kissed her – "I'm going down for some coffee, wow! What a dream. If I could control what I dream about, I would have that again." The seed was replanted and he left the room.

7:10 – AM

At the same time at another home in University Gardens Ana sat in a quandary. It has been less than a week since Sharon's passing and she is not sure how soon is too soon to let Jean-Pierre know her feelings for him. She wants to comfort him the way a woman comforts a man. Ana truly felt sad about Sharon, but it must be a sign that this is fate. A triumphant smile began to form as she mulled over the idea – 'he is mine'.

About the Author

W.L. Samuel is still as adventurous as he was in his last book. His fascination with helicopters has pushed him to the decision of adding achieving a PPLH to his list of personal goals.

Printed in the United States
By Bookmasters